"What if I could find a husband for you, a man who would agree to a marriage short-term, while Gus gets back on his feet?"

Shannon's eyes widened. "Are you serious?"

Jackson swallowed. Was he? "Yeah."

"Who?"

"Me."

She jumped up and was out the door in record time. She needed air. She needed a clear head. And what she didn't need was the black-eyed Cajun following her.

"Gee, Shannon," Jackson said as he caught up to her. "You sure know how to make a guy feel good about his proposal."

"That wasn't a proposal, that was a—" She gulped past the confusion in her throat.

"What scares you more, Shannon? That you won't be able to pretend you love me? Or that you never stopped loving me to begin with?"

Dear Reader,

Whether you're enjoying one of the first snowfalls of the season or lounging in a beach chair at some plush island resort, I hope you've got some great books by your side. I'm especially excited about the Silhouette Romance titles this month as we're kicking off 2006 with two great new miniseries by some of your all-time favorite authors.

Cara Colter teams up with her daughter, Cassidy Caron, to launch our new PERPETUALLY YOURS trilogy. *In Love's Nine Lives* (#1798) a beautiful librarian's extremely possessive tabby tries to thwart a budding romance between *his* mistress and a man who seems all wrong for her but is anything but. Teresa Southwick returns with *That Touch of Pink* (#1799)—the first in her BUY-A-GUY trilogy. When a single mom literally buys a former military man at a bachelor auction to help her daughter earn a wilderness badge, she gets a lot more than she bargained for...and is soon earning points toward *her own* romantic survival badge. Old sparks turn into an all-out blaze when the hero returns to the family ranch in *Sometimes When We Kiss* (#1800) by Linda Goodnight. Finally, Elise Mayr debuts with *The Rancher's Redemption* (#1801) in which a widow, desperate to help her sick daughter, throws herself on the mercy of her commanding brother-in-law whose eyes reflect anything but the hate she'd expected.

And be sure to come back next month for more great reading, with Sandra Paul's distinctive addition to the PERPETUALLY YOURS trilogy and Judy Christenberry's new madcap mystery.

Have a very happy and healthy 2006.

Ann Leslie Tuttle
Associate Senior Editor

Please address questions and book requests to:
Silhouette Reader Service
U.S.: 3010 Walden Ave., P.O. Box 1325, Buffalo, NY 14269
Canadian: P.O. Box 609, Fort Erie, Ont. L2A 5X3

LINDA GOODNIGHT
SOMETIMES WHEN WE KISS

SILHOUETTE *Romance*®

Published by Silhouette Books

America's Publisher of Contemporary Romance

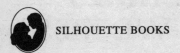

SILHOUETTE BOOKS

ISBN 0-373-19800-0

SOMETIMES WHEN WE KISS

Copyright © 2006 by Linda Goodnight

This edition published by arrangement with Harlequin Books S.A.

® and TM are trademarks of Harlequin Books S.A., used under license. Trademarks indicated with ® are registered in the United States Patent and Trademark Office, the Canadian Trade Marks Office and in other countries.

Visit Silhouette Books at www.eHarlequin.com

Printed in U.S.A.

Books by Linda Goodnight

Silhouette Romance

LINDA GOODNIGHT

A romantic at heart, Linda Goodnight believes in the traditional values of family and home. Writing books enables her to share her certainty that, with faith and perseverance, love can last forever and happy endings really are possible.

A native of Oklahoma, Linda lives in the country with her husband, Gene, and Mugsy, an adorably obnoxious rat terrier. She and Gene have a blended family of six grown children. An elementary school teacher, she is also a licensed nurse. When time permits, Linda loves to read, watch football and rodeo, and indulge in chocolate. She also enjoys taking long, calorie-burning walks in the nearby woods. Readers can write to her at linda@lindagoodnight.com, or c/o Silhouette Books, 233 Broadway, Suite 1001, New York, NY 10279.

To Western artist and horse trainer Nadine Meade
for inspiration, advice and just plain old
being a good neighbor.

Chapter One

Riding a horse was like riding a bicycle. If you fell off, you had to get right back on again.

Backhanding the dirt from her eyes, Shannon Wyoming stuck one booted foot into the stirrup, grabbed the saddle horn and vaulted onto one of the few horses that did not understand that she could—and would—break him to ride.

Never mind that her backside would be black and blue, Shannon never allowed anything to get the best of her.

For one glorious moment Shannon thought she had finally succeeded, that Domino's stubborn spirit had broken. He crow-hopped across the sunlit arena, all four legs stiff, back arched higher than a Halloween cat as he bounced. Crow-hopping was a piece of cake to an experienced trainer like Shannon. No problem. He'd settle down in a minute.

Fifteen seconds into the ride, Domino changed tactics. His hind legs shot out behind him and the bronc went into a wild bucking exposition that would have unseated a rodeo champ. When Shannon leaned back to compensate, he yanked his head down hard, unbalancing her. One more wild gyration and she flew off with all the projection of a human cannonball, but with considerably less grace.

She landed facedown, the hard-packed dirt of the arena knocking the breath from her. No belly buster from a rope swing at Coyote Creek ever hurt this bad.

She lay there in the Texas sun with not a desire in the world to get up, hoping breath would return before her heart stopped. Domino, as she well knew, wouldn't come anywhere near for a while. He was likely in the corner of the lot, sulking.

Gnats buzzed around her ears and one pesky horsefly threatened to add insult to injury, so she had to get up. She sucked in a mouthful of arena dirt, then opened her eyes. The first thing she saw was a pair of dusty, well-worn boots—snakeskin boots—crossed at the ankle in a posture of total relaxation. Equally worn blue jeans, made long the way cowboys like them, bunched softly atop the brown boots.

Great. She'd not only been thrown like a greenhorn, but she had a witness to verify her humiliation.

Stifling an inward groan that had as much to do with her unwanted visitor as with her state of breathlessness,

Shannon pushed up from the ground. She slapped at her jeans and shirt, loosing a dust storm that obscured her vision and threatened her already tortured air passages. She wiped a dirty sleeve across her face and squinted toward the fence rail where a cowboy leaned, indolently watching her.

Every nerve in Shannon's body sprang to full alert. A lightning strike would not have shocked her more.

Jackson Kane. When had he come back to Rattlesnake? And what was he doing here, on her ranch, where he was not a welcome guest?

He didn't look much different than he had the last time she'd seen him, though her carefully preserved pride would not let her go there again, even in memory. Tall and wide-shouldered, his dark and sexy looks still did funny things to her insides and infuriated her to the point of rudeness. She didn't want to talk to him, even now, didn't want to notice the way his incredibly sexy mouth wallowed a narrow piece of straw, didn't want to notice the new age lines around his Cajun black eyes.

But she noticed. Darn it. She noticed.

"What do you want?" She slammed her hands on her hips in a fit of annoyance.

He grinned then, slow and lazy and insolent, as if he knew how much he affected her by showing up out of the blue after all this time.

Taking the straw from between his teeth, he studied her long enough to set her heart to racing and to send the heat of a blush creeping up her neck.

He aimed the piece of straw at her, and she saw then that what she'd thought was straw was actually a tiny lollipop.

She burst out laughing. "A Dum-Dum sucker. How appropriate."

He pushed off the fence and strutted toward her in that loose-hipped, rolling gait of a man who'd spent plenty of time on a horse and was comfortable in his own skin. Digging in his shirt pocket, he extracted another candy and thrust it toward her. "Want one?"

She eyed the treat with suspicion. "Your idea of a peace offering?"

"Do I need a peace offering?"

She snatched the sucker from his outstretched hand. "It'll take more than this."

One side of his mouth kicked up and a dimple deep enough to swim in winked at her. "Then give it back."

Like the kid she'd been when Jackson Kane had broken her heart and left her with enough guilty regrets to last a lifetime, Shannon ripped off the paper and shoved the sucker into her mouth. A burst of syrupy cherry didn't do a thing to sweeten her mood.

"Some things, once taken, can't ever be given back, Jackson, or had you forgotten?"

Her jibe wiped the grin off his face. Good. She didn't want him having fun at her expense. Not anymore. Because the things she'd given him—and lost because of him—were far too painful to joke about.

Spinning away from his disturbing presence, Shannon searched for her hat. Domino stood in the corner near the barn entrance, eyeing her with caution. The Texas morning was heating up and a bead of sweat tickled the back of her neck. She slapped at a gnat that found the sweat enticing.

"Looking for that?"

Jackson aimed the Dum-Dum at what had once been a nice white, rather pricey Resistol, lying crumpled in the dirt not three yards from him. A gentleman would have picked it up for her, but not Jackson. He stood there with that 'possum-eatin' grin on his face and mischief in his eyes while she stormed across the paddock. Domino, that worthless piece of horseflesh, had taken his frustrations out on her new hat.

With the crumbled straw in hand, she turned her attention to the horse. Mad as he made her, Domino wasn't really worthless. Doc Everts was paying a nice price to have his new mount trained at the Circle W Ranch. Moving quietly, she went to the animal, took the dragging reins and led him out of the paddock and away from Jackson Kane, taking the memories of their past along with her.

"Hey, Shan!"

Shannon's shoulders slumped. The thud of boots against hard ground warned her of his approach. She should have known he wouldn't be that easy to get rid of. After ten years, he was bound to have a reason for showing up this way.

"Don't let the gate hit you in the backside on your way out," she called over one shoulder.

He caught up to her. "I take it you're still mad."

Incredulous, she stopped in the entrance of the shadowy barn. Standing right next to her this way, he looked gigantic. She'd forgotten how tall he was, how he dwarfed her completely. As a love-struck teenager she'd felt so protected by his size. As an adult she was unnerved.

"You are amazing, you know that?" She gave him her frostiest glare.

Eyes brightening, he pumped his eyebrows. "That's what they tell me."

"That was not a compliment." She swung around to face him, caught a whiff of grape sucker and a certain manly something that was Jackson Kane and no one else. "Why are you here, Jackson?"

Without a word, he took the reins from her and led the paint into a stall where he began the task of unsaddling. Dumbfounded, Shannon followed, taking refuge in the familiar scents of alfalfa hay and sweet-feed and leather tack.

"I asked you a fair question."

"All right then." He looked up from loosening the cinch and wallowed the sucker to one corner of his mouth. Shannon struggled not to follow the action, but lost that battle. His talented mouth had always fascinated her.

"Your granddad thought you could use some help out here. I was available so he hired me."

"You? Available? What happened to the rodeo circuit?" She refused to acknowledge the part about him being hired. Not to work for her, he wasn't. And she'd tell Granddad that herself.

"All my rowdy friends have settled down." He grimaced as if the admission pained him no end, then dragged the saddle off the prancing horse and tossed it over a saddletree. "So I've retired."

"Why don't you go back to Louisiana?"

"Nobody there I know anymore. Most of my kin are gone, except for Aunt Bonnie. And she's here in Rattlesnake."

Shannon knew Jackson's great-aunt Bonnie, a feisty twig of a lady, whose husband had died a couple of years ago. She worked at the grocery store in Rattlesnake, though she must be up in her seventies by now.

"I thought," Jackson went on, "my aunt could use a relative close by, and Jett and Colt figured work wouldn't be hard to find."

Opening the stall door, he led the horse forward and waited for the animal to head, bucking and kicking up dust, into the open corral. Sunshine gleamed on the black and white hide.

"Then go to work for them." Colt and Jett were the Garret brothers, two former rodeo cowboys who owned the largest ranch in the panhandle. Jackson and Jett had been traveling partners until an injury had forced Jett to retire from the circuit. "I don't need you or want you on the Circle W."

"Look, Shannon, can't we let bygones be bygones?

We were kids back then. Kids," he added again with emphasis. "I didn't realize I'd hurt you."

She stiffened. "You didn't hurt me. You made me mad. No one had ever jilted me before."

"Who said I jilted you?"

"What other term do you use when a guy calls a girl and says, 'I'll catch you later, darlin',' and then never does?"

"Shannon." His voice fell to that honeyed baritone that had talked her into too many things. To her total amazement and eternal discomfort, he stroked one finger down her cheek. "Don't be mad."

How was it that she hadn't seen this man in nearly ten years and yet, he could stroll back into her life, and she felt as though he'd never left?

Yes, they'd been kids, foolish, imprudent teenagers who hadn't considered the consequences of their actions. He was a rodeo cowboy so she'd known he wouldn't stick around, and she'd promised herself not to be hurt once he was gone. And she wouldn't have been, except for what he'd left behind.

"All that happened a very long time ago, Jackson. I'm not mad. I'm not hurt. I've simply grown up and moved on."

"Then why the chilly reception?"

"Maybe I was surprised to see you after all this time."

He laughed, appreciating the ironic understatement. "Maybe."

"I'm too busy with the future to revisit the past, so if

you don't mind. . ." She waved a hand around at the small ranch, the barns, the corrals, the modest brick house snuggled between two thick pines. "I have work to do."

"Show me the way."

"Excuse me?"

"Work is why I'm here, remember? Your granddad hired me?"

Shannon stewed over that little piece of information. Though she'd grown up here, her grandfather was the true owner of this place. But since his heart attack six months ago he'd let her call the shots. That he'd hired Jackson Kane irked her no end, but they'd been thinking of taking on a hand and Granddad couldn't know that Jackson would be a problem for her. After all, their brief fling had happened a long time ago.

Yes, she needed more help now that Granddad was no longer able to carry his weight, but Jackson? She didn't think so.

"Then perhaps you should get your duties from him. I don't need you."

Jackson removed the lollipop from his mouth and studied the now empty stick. "He said you needed some help breaking these new colts and from the looks of that paint, I'd say he was right."

"I stayed on him way more than eight seconds. In a rodeo arena, I'd have won money. Would you have?"

"Guess we'll have to find out."

"Guess we won't," she said with a hint of mocking

sarcasm. "Breaking the horses is my job. I'm the trainer. And that paint happens to be a special case, more difficult than most, but I promised his owner he'd end up as gentle as a dog. I'll keep that promise no matter how long it takes."

"There are new techniques available. Have you tried any of them?"

She shifted, uncomfortable under the growing heat and annoying buzz of buffalo gnats as well as his assumption that her training techniques were lacking.

"What are you? A horse whisperer or something?"

His mouth kicked up and brought with it that insolent dimple. "Maybe."

"Well, I happen to know what I'm doing. Granddad taught me to break horses from the time I could ride. His methods worked then and they work now. I don't need some rodeo cowboy turned horse psychologist to tell me how a horse thinks and why he behaves the way he does. Breaking that paint is a matter of wearing him down."

"Mind if I give him a try?"

"Yes. As a matter of fact, I do mind." So what if he'd spent most of his life riding broncs, both saddle and bareback. He wasn't a trainer. He was a rodeo performer. She could do this job better.

He shrugged. "Have it your way, but you're paying me a salary whether I do anything or not."

"Consider yourself unhired."

"Sorry." He didn't look one bit contrite. "Your granddaddy hired me. He's the only one who can fire me."

Shannon rolled her eyes heavenward. "I need to have a talk with my grandfather."

Jackson slouched against the paddock gate, unwrapped another Dum-Dum—a green one this time—and shot her his cockiest smile. "Go ahead. I'll wait here."

Jackson tipped his hat back and watched her go, admiring the cute little jiggle of her perfect backside encased in tight jeans. The worn spot between the pockets where she'd spent hours in the saddle was especially appealing. Not that he'd tell sweet Shannon that. She'd likely punch him in the nose.

She'd changed in ten years. And he sure wasn't complaining about that. At eighteen she'd been a girl, fresh as the outdoors and full of promise. The promise had been fulfilled. Today she was all woman, rounded in the right spots, and full of vinegar. He liked a little fire and sass in a woman. Shannon with her blue eyes and sun-blond hair barely reached his shirt pocket, but she could definitely hold her own. He looked forward to reminiscing in a more practical manner.

But first he'd have to get past that bad attitude she had toward him, a reaction that surprised him. He'd had no idea he'd left a burr under her saddle. Sure, they'd played around back then, had a good time, but it wasn't as if they'd been in love. Love? He almost shivered in spite of the warm day. They'd only spent a summer together, and at nineteen he hadn't known diddly about love. To tell the truth, he was nearly thirty and he still didn't know anything about the troublesome emotion. Didn't want to know either.

What he did know about was horses. And her grandfather had sense enough to know that if he was ever going to expand his training and breaking facility he needed a top-notch trainer. Shannon may not like change, but her ideas were as antiquated as a crank telephone. He, on the other hand, had spent years studying under the best so-called horse whisperers, gleaning their techniques, adding some of his own. And he was good, though only a few knew it—so far.

During his rodeo years he'd helped other cowboys with rank mounts, but he'd had no real chance to prove himself in a larger capacity. That was all about to change.

From the moment he'd discovered Aunt Bonnie's financial troubles, he'd made up his mind to come back to Rattlesnake and help out. After all, she'd been there for him when he was four years old and his mother had jumped ship, leaving his bewildered father to raise a child alone. The kicker was Bonnie was his dad's aunt, not his, but she'd rearranged her entire life to raise him. She'd tossed over her job and had even waited to marry until Jackson was a teenager and old enough to look out for himself. He owed her big time.

He didn't have a lot of money, but regardless of what he had to do, nobody was foreclosing on his aunt's small home.

This job would help. And it would also propel him

toward his dream. Though he'd shared the vision with no one else in case he fell on his face like a fool, Jackson had a dream that had kept him going for a long time. Someday, he'd run his own symposia on horse training and people would come from all over the country to have Jackson Kane teach them his methods. He'd take the rankest horses in the land and turn them into docile pets, well-disciplined ranch animals or fine rodeo stock.

In the meantime, he'd find a way to save Aunt Bonnie's home and make sure she was well taken care of in her old age. That was the least he could do.

The paint gelding Shannon had called Domino wandered back toward the arena, anxiously eyeing the cowboy but clearly hoping to make his way back inside the shady barn. Jackson gnawed at the sour-apple candy and held back a smile. Old Domino had a weakness. He wondered if Shannon had noticed.

Emitting a low whistle, he waited for the horse's reaction. As he suspected, the paint stopped dead still, flicked his ears forward and winded the strange cowboy.

Patience. That's what a trainer needed with a horse like Domino. So Jackson leaned against the iron gate, relaxed but watchful, waiting for the horse to come to him.

He didn't have to wait long. The gelding, tail swishing at flies, ears twitching, lowered his head and plodded toward him.

Jackson extended a hand to stroke the warm, smooth neck and inhaled the rich, animal scent. His chest strained toward contentment.

Yep. This was where he needed to be. Right here where horses were already boarded and ready to train, a ranch with a good, solid reputation. And regardless of Shannon's attitude or resistance, Jackson Kane was here to stay. At least for the time being.

Shannon knew better than to slam the door. Although she was a grown woman, Granddad would send her back outside and make her close the door like a lady. So even if she didn't feel much like a lady right now, she paused inside the office door and took three cleansing breaths.

Her grandfather looked up. "What's got you in a snit?"

So much for her efforts at self-control. "I'm not in a snit, but we do need to talk. Why didn't you tell me you'd hired Jackson Kane to work for us?"

Her grandfather laid aside his reading glasses and pinched the bridge of his nose. Since his heart attack, he'd aged, and though he was seventy, Shannon had always considered him a rock until now. She'd been three when her parents had died in a car wreck and her widowed grandfather had taken her to raise. He was all the family she'd ever known and the thought of losing him scared her half to death.

Now she worried about him constantly. Nagged him to eat better, to rest more, and not to worry over her and the ranch. But she knew he did anyway.

"Now that I'm a useless old goat," he said, "you've got to have some help around here."

"But why Jackson?"

"Why not? He's a cowboy, a mighty fine horseman, and seems like an honest enough feller."

"How can you possibly know all that about a man who's practically a stranger?"

"Colt Garret."

"Oh." Granddad would trust Colt Garret with his life. If Colt vouched for Jackson, her grandfather wouldn't blink an eye about handing him the keys to the ranch.

She tried a new tack. "I'm the horse trainer. I don't need him."

"Now, Shannon, the man's studied under John Lyons and you know dang well Lyons is the best there is. Horse breakin' and trainin' is a rough job, a man's job. Why not let Jackson take over the horses so you can concentrate on running the business end of things. You're a whale of a lot better at figures and purchasing than I am."

"A man's job!" Shannon hadn't heard another word after that little jab. Of all the insults, she hated that one the most. A female doing a man's job. All her life she'd battled ignorant horsemen who thought she should be more worried about breaking a nail than breaking a horse. Her pulse picked up. Anger lifted the hairs on her arms.

Granddad must have seen the fury in her. He raised a gnarled hand. "I won't argue about this. Kane is hired and that's that."

All the blood in her body rushed to her head. "And I won't allow it."

"Now, Shannon—" Granddad stood up, reaching toward her, his tone cajoling. But he'd no more than found his feet when the outstretched hand grabbed for his chest.

"Granddad!" Argument forgotten in concern for the only parent she'd ever known, Shannon rushed forward to wrap her arms around him. "Is it your heart? Are you in pain?"

"Need to sit," he managed, short of breath to the point of gasping. "My pills."

Shannon took his arm and, frightened by the cold and clammy skin beneath her fingers, eased him onto the chair. Then she searched frantically through the desk for his medication, discovering the bottle at last beneath a stack of papers.

She shook out a pill, placed the tiny white tablet under his tongue and waited. From the looks of the bottle, this wasn't the first episode of pain, but it was the first she'd witnessed.

"Should I call an ambulance? Or take you to the hospital?"

Eyes closed, he shook his head. "Get Kane."

Kane? The request startled her. Why would he ask for Jackson? A sudden jolt of understanding exploded adrenaline into her bloodstream. Granddad thought he might be dying and didn't want her to be alone.

Terrified to leave him for even a moment, Shannon had no choice. She raced to the back door and screamed out. "Jackson. Hurry. Granddad is sick!"

Waiting only long enough to see the tall Cajun jerk

away from the gate and start in a long lope for the house, Shannon rushed back into the office and to her grandfather.

She sank to the floor beside his chair and laid her head against his knee as she'd done a thousand times growing up. Then the action had been to seek comfort from an anchor of a man who had all the answers. Now she needed to be the comforter, the strong one.

Please, God, don't let me lose him. I'll never argue with him again. Ever. If hiring Jackson makes him happy, I won't say another word against him.

The squeak of the storm door and pound of boot steps heralded Jackson's entry. If she hadn't been so frightened, she might have been amused. For a big guy, he moved pretty fast.

He stormed into the room, expression concerned but confident. Shannon breathed an undeniable sigh of relief. She didn't want to face this alone and somehow Jackson's quiet strength gave her courage.

"What happened?"

"His heart. He had a heart attack about six months ago. He's been on medication ever since."

"Hospital," Granddad managed to say through pale lips, though his eyes remained closed.

Jackson never hesitated. "Get the SUV," he said to Shannon. "I'll meet you at the back door."

Then he scooped her grandfather into his arms as if he were a small child instead of a hundred-and-sixty-pound adult.

Grabbing the keys from the hook on the wall, Shannon raced for the truck.

By the time she pulled around back, Jackson was waiting. She bolted out of the driver's seat and opened the back door, helping Jackson ease Granddad onto the empty bench seat. She started to close the door, but Jackson stopped her with a hand on her arm.

"You ride back here with him. I'll drive."

Unused to taking orders from anyone, Shannon wanted to argue, but the situation was too serious, and he was right. She needed to be with her grandfather. Any fool could drive. Even Jackson Kane.

Chapter Two

Jackson stood in the waiting room sucking in the unmistakable odor of antiseptic and sick people as he listened to a white-coated lady doctor explaining Gus Wyoming's heart condition to Shannon. He'd rather smell the back end of a horse any day than the inside of a hospital.

He shifted from one boot to the other and wished for a dip of snuff, though he'd broken that habit more than two years ago. He hated hospitals. Nearly everyone he ever knew who'd gone into one never came out alive—Jett Garret being the exception. And look what had happened to him. Jackson suppressed a shudder. His poor buddy had gone to the hospital and had ended up losing his dream. Never mind that he was deliriously happy with the cute little nurse he'd found there. Jackson couldn't imagine anything worse than giving up the dream—especially for a creature as undependable as a woman.

"Your grandfather has some blockage in his carotid arteries," he heard the doctor say and focused his full attention in that direction.

"Is that what causes his chest pain?"

"Yes. And the blockage also causes the shortness of breath when he overexerts himself." The doctor removed a pair of wire-rimmed glasses and cleaned them against her coat. "If Mr. Wyoming had seen a doctor when he first began experiencing symptoms…" She stopped and shook her head, apparently seeing the futility in what-might-have-beens. "He doesn't follow doctor's orders very well."

Shannon smiled, though Jackson could see the worry hanging on her like a wet saddle blanket—heavy and miserable. She'd been unfaltering since the moment they tore away from the ranch, her strength and constant upbeat chatter in the back seat of the SUV making the trip into town much calmer for him as well as the old man. There would be no hysterics from this little cowgirl.

Regardless of her sexy, all-woman looks, Shannon Wyoming was as tough as a pine knot. Always had been, but in the years since he'd seen her, she'd grown stronger. She had a set to her chin and steely determination in her blue eyes that said she wouldn't give up and she wouldn't give in. Much as he hated to admit it, he admired that. Almost as much as he admired her round little backside in a pair of tight jeans.

Her voice and his own common sense yanked him back into the conversation. Better not let Shannon catch him eyeing her behind.

"That's Granddad. He doesn't take orders well from anyone."

Like his granddaughter, Jackson thought. He shoved off the wall and moved up beside her. "Is he going to need surgery?"

The doctor looked from Shannon to the dark cowboy, her expression questioning.

"This is Jackson Kane," Shannon said. "Our... He works for my grandfather and me."

She'd finally admitted he had the job, but Jackson felt no victory in her saying so. If Gus couldn't carry on as always, she'd be stuck with her new hired hand whether she liked the idea or not. He'd have to deal with her reluctance if his own dreams were to come true.

"Not right now. And if he will do the things I tell him, maybe never. With the right medications we may be able to clear out the blockage or at least part of it. But he needs to make some significant lifestyle changes."

Jackson knew that wouldn't set well with a man like Gus, and from the way Shannon fidgeted she knew it, too.

"How can we help?" He didn't know why he felt compelled to see Shannon through this. Her family, her grandfather was not his business. But the anxiety around Shannon's mouth gave him the most irrational desire to kiss away her troubles and tell her everything would be all right. Must be a flashback to the good times they'd had when they were randy teenagers.

With a concerted effort, he drew his attention away from Shannon's mouth and back to the doctor.

The doctor replaced her glasses. "How does your grandfather handle his stress?"

"Handle it?" Shannon huffed. "He doesn't. He keeps everything bottled up inside so I won't worry about it."

Jackson could have told them that. Holding trouble inside was the cowboy way. Although lots of men blew off steam by getting drunk on Saturday night or picking a barroom fight, Gus wasn't the type. Maybe he had been in his younger days, but not now, not even ten years ago.

"I thought you might say that. While caused by the blockage, his blood-pressure problem is exacerbated by the stress," said the tiny doctor. "You need to do everything possible to eliminate any areas of tension in his life."

Shannon frowned, a cute little pucker between her eyes that gave Jackson the strangest desire to slip an arm around her waist and pull her close.

"That is not going to be easy." She gnawed on her full bottom lip and danged if he didn't start staring at her mouth again.

"No, I don't expect it will be. But if Mr. Wyoming is to regain optimal health, he must reduce stress and control his blood pressure. If he behaves himself, he could very well beat this thing. Otherwise, he is looking at some serious complications in the not-too-distant future."

Shannon swallowed hard, her face blanching. "I can't let anything happen to my granddad."

"Nothing's going to happen to Gus," Jackson said. "We'll see to it."

At his reassurance, Shannon relaxed a little and got that determined jut to her chin. "Okay. You're right. We are going to get him well. I can handle the business side of the ranch, keep him from seeing any financial problems." She turned to Jackson. "Jackson, don't tell Granddad about any problems with the horses or their owners. Okay?"

Lying to a man he respected was not what Jackson had in mind. A man who spent his life working on a ranch, burning his muscles into exhaustion wouldn't take kindly to two women plotting his retirement to a rockin' chair by hiding things from him. And if Gus could hear this conversation, he would be one unhappy cowboy.

"Gus's nobody's fool."

"I'd be the first to agree with that. But I don't want to lose him either. For the sake of his health, we absolutely have to keep him relaxed. So gloss over any problems, only tell him the good things." She placed a hand on his arm and his pulse rate kicked like a young mule. "Please, Jackson. I need your help."

When she looked so worried like that, her blue eyes threatening a rainstorm, he was helpless to argue.

"I thought you wanted to fire me."

She crossed her arms, an action that pushed the front

of her tank top up and out. A man could totally lose his concentration at such a sight.

"Don't rub it in."

A devilish impulse made him tease. "Admit you're glad I'm here, and I won't."

The good doctor, whom Jackson had completely forgotten, cleared her throat. "If you two will excuse me, I have rounds to make. We'll talk again before Mr. Wyoming is discharged."

She bustled away, pager beeping at her waist, nurses armed with charts following her down the long white corridor.

"Seems like a good doctor."

"She's terribly overworked, but yes, I trust her." Wearily she pushed her hair behind one ear. "If Dr. Torrence says Granddad will get well faster if he eats right and isn't stressed, then I have to find ways to keep him content."

"We."

"Pardon?"

"Didn't you just admit you need my help?"

Her eyes lit up and two parentheses appeared around her full, kissable lips. "You win. I'll take your offer of help."

"Wait, I wasn't finished." He couldn't resist the urge to goad.

She cocked an eyebrow. "Well?"

"Admit you're glad I'm here."

She rolled her eyes. "Okay, Jackson. I'm glad you're here. Are you happy now?"

"A little insincere, but it will do."

Jackson had the sudden thought that he might be in trouble. He didn't know why he cared, but he wanted her to want him here. And that worried him more than a little.

A few minutes later, Shannon headed to the coronary care unit to see her granddad. Jackson, bless him, made noises about phoning his aunt, but she recognized the effort to give her time alone with her grandfather. Now she wished he'd come along; she needed a referee.

"I wouldn't mind dying so much if you was settled." Propped up at a forty-five-degree angle, Granddad had tossed off the oxygen mask the minute she'd walked in. Though he sounded a bit winded, his will hadn't weakened at all.

How was she supposed to keep him calm when he had such a one-track mind? "I am settled, Granddad. And you are not going to die."

"Everybody dies, little girl. Even cranky old mavericks like me." He shifted sideways in the bed, looking old and withered beneath the stark white sheets. "But don't go changing the subject on me. I ain't talkin' about me. I'm talkin' about you and this problem you have with finding a man and settling down."

"I have everything in the world I want or need including a good man—you."

He waved a hand in impatience, dismissing her statement as nonsense. "That ain't what I mean and you know it. You need a husband, but ever time a prospect comes along, you lope off like a green-broke colt."

"Men don't interest me that much."

"A few of 'em interested you enough to get engaged." He screwed up his brow in thought. "How many fellers have you run off? I've lost count."

He made her sound like one of those Hollywood types who ran through men faster than cold beer on a hot day. She took exception to that.

"Only three." Three broken engagements, the last one less than six months ago. Each time, as soon as the commitment was made, she'd gotten cold feet. Instead of a ring on her finger, Shannon had felt as if they'd wanted to put a noose around her neck.

"Seems like more than that to me." He coughed, a wheezy noise that worried Shannon.

She gave him a drink of water, waited for him to regain his breath before asking, "Are you all right?"

"Won't be until I know you have someone to take care of you when I'm gone."

Her voice rose in frustration. "You're not going anywhere."

"Yes, I am. Margaret's been waiting for thirty years and she never was a patient woman. I'll hear about it for a month once I get over there so I need to quit procrastinating and get on with it. She's just like you. Once she gets over her snit, we'll be the happiest pair in paradise."

Shannon knew he was trying to make her laugh, to make a joke out of dying, but she saw no humor in losing the man who'd loved her and provided for her ever since she could remember.

"Stop it, Granddad. Just stop it. I need you. The ranch needs you."

"What you need is a good man to look after you, so when I do go I can rest in peace instead of wondering if you're all right."

So they were back to that again. All three of her engagements had been as much to please him as to please herself. But every single fiancé had wanted to run her life, as well as her ranch. As soon as the engagement had been announced, they'd expected her to become someone else, to give up her hard work on the ranch and become a lady of the manor. And she wasn't having any of that. She could ride, rope, train horses and run a ranch better than any man on the planet. She could stand on her own two feet, thank you. Shannon Gayle Wyoming did not need a man.

"Granddad, the doctor says you can live with this heart problem if you'll only learn to behave yourself better and stop stressing over the small stuff."

"Small stuff? My granddaughter's happiness is not small. I likely *could* get back on my pegs if I wasn't so all-fired worried about your future."

Guilt as heavy as a feed truck descended on Shannon. She'd always been Granddad's first and foremost concern, and she hated being the cause of his worry. To think that she was keeping him from getting well was just too much.

Sitting down on the pristine sheets, Shannon

wrapped one hand around her grandfather's gnarled fingers. "Granddad, I promise you I will seriously consider finding the right man."

"When?"

She hedged. "Soon."

"What about this Kane fellow? I like him. He's a good horseman."

"Granddad!" Shannon shot a quick glance toward the door, thankful no one, especially not Jackson, was in sight. She could hardly believe Granddad had said such a thing. Why, Jackson had only just arrived and already Granddad was pushing the two of them together. "What are you thinking?"

"Well," Gus said, feigning innocence. "He ain't married. I asked him."

Shaking her head, she laughed. "Did you really?"

"Ah, only in the course of hiring him. I wasn't trying to fix you up or nothing."

She breathed an inward sigh of relief. "Thank goodness. I can do that for myself."

The last thing she needed was a matchmaking grandparent. Especially when it came to Jackson Kane.

Long ago she'd taken that painful summer, locked the memory in a closet inside her mind, and tried not to visit there too often. Occasionally, like today with Jackson so ever present, the memory sneaked out, but she'd learned to skirt around it, not look too close, and shove it back inside as quickly as possible. Remembering what-might-have-been hurt too much.

"Well, he ain't half-bad is he?" Granddad was rattling on. "I mean, he's decent looking. He knows horses. And he's clean."

"Clean?" Latching onto the silly notion, she giggled. If she were to make a list of characteristics for a potential husband, would this one have made the list? "Clean?"

Gus chuckled and pulled her into the hook of his arm.

At that moment, the door swooshed open, and Mr. Clean himself entered the room. Half-inclined on her grandfather's side, Shannon looked up and burst out laughing.

With a puzzled grin, Jackson glanced behind him then ambled into the room. He reached into his pocket and pulled out the now familiar Dum-Dum.

Granddad was right. He was definitely clean. The smell of his morning shower swirled in the door with him.

She couldn't help noticing the strong, dark, *clean* hands unwrapping the orange sucker or their graceful, effortless movements. She loved his hands, had always admired those hands that could hold a thrashing horse with an iron grip, but could also hold her with such tenderness.

The paper crumpled into his fist and that tiny sound startled her to awareness. Good golly, Miss Molly. What was she thinking? And why?

But she knew the answer to that. Granddad's silly nonsense had her noticing that Jackson Kane was much more than clean. He was cowboy sexy and more attractive than a man had a right to be.

Looking at him stirred some primal urge Shannon hadn't felt in a long time. Ten years to be exact.

Her heart thudded in her throat until she wondered if she was the one with the heart problem instead of Granddad.

With his talk of seeing her settled with a good man, and her desperate need to make him happy, Granddad had her thinking things she shouldn't.

Insanely ridiculous thoughts that she'd never allowed before danced through her mind.

Though the subject had never been broached, what if she had married Jackson back then? What if he'd known about the baby? Would he have asked her to marry him? Would she have agreed?

Pushing up from Granddad's hug, she turned her back to Jackson and began to straighten the bedside table. Her hands shook and she was acutely aware that her odd behavior created curiosity in the two men.

Shannon had been certain she'd settled this issue years ago, but Granddad's inadvertent teasing said the problem of Jackson Kane was a long way from being over.

Chapter Three

One month later, life on the Circle W had returned to some semblance of normality. To Shannon's relief, Gus, though straining at the bit, was trying hard to follow doctor's orders. Except for the thirty-minute prescribed walk he took each morning, he mostly puttered around in the house, grumbling about old age and bossy granddaughters.

True to his word, Jackson had gone above and beyond the amount of pay he received as assistant trainer. Long after he should have gone home to his aunt Bonnie's house in Rattlesnake, he worked on the ranch tending to things that he knew would bother Gus if left undone.

"You gonna stand there and stare at me or get acquainted with this new colt?"

At Jackson's amused voice, Shannon realized she had indeed been staring at him.

Morning looked good on him, she thought, noting that he'd come quickly when she'd called with the news that the mare was in labor. The moisture of his morning shower still glistened on his inky-black hair and the clean, fresh scent of soap and shaving cream amounted to sensory overload.

They were inside a stall in one of the horse barns to do the all-important job of imprinting a newborn foal. Jackson had arrived only moments before the mare delivered the new baby. They'd watched while the tiny bay had suckled and bonded with his mother, then lay down to sleep. That la-la land between sleep and wakefulness was the perfect time to handle a new colt.

The scene of mother and baby was as moving now as it had been the first time she'd experienced it. She always felt softer, more feminine somehow, after witnessing the miracle of birth. For some reason, having Jackson in the stall intensified the feelings.

Shannon went down on her knees beside the animal. "Hand me that brush on the wall behind you. I'll stroke his withers and sides while you handle his head."

Petting, rubbing and brushing, Shannon and Jackson worked to imprint the colt so that he would not be afraid of humans. Shannon was acutely aware of the movement of Jackson's muscular shoulders as he caressed the animal's ears and face. Longing, totally unwanted, shimmied through her.

More than once in their month of working side by side, awareness had simmered between them. This morning was no different.

"How you doing with Domino?" he asked, voice quiet in the dark, musty-scented barn.

"He's coming along," she hedged. What a lie. Domino was not cooperating. After more than a month, he could be ridden, but he had no manners and wasn't safe for most people to ride.

"Need any help?" *Stroke, rub. Touch. Caress.*

The shiver went over Shannon again. She had to stop looking at his hands. Still rotating the brush over the brown hide, she looked up at his face instead. Big mistake. Eyes like fudge sauce studied her. Little sparks of lightning shot off beneath her skin.

"No, I do not need help." To cover her other, less certain feelings, she chose to feign annoyance. "I've told you before. I know how to train a horse better than any horse whisperer. Domino has to learn who is boss and I can teach him that."

"I'd sure like to get my hands on him."

Pure stubborn pride made her say, "Forget it. You have plenty of other horses to train."

She probably could use some help from Jackson. He was good, excellent even. And she had grown to depend on him. She looked forward to his arrival each morning and enjoyed working with him all day. And if she felt an extra burst of energy in his presence or if she noticed how clean and masculine he smelled, well, so what.

She was a woman. He was definitely a man. And her grandfather was putting irrational thoughts in her head on a daily basis.

Jackson, seeing the futility of arguing with her, changed the subject. "So how's Gus this morning?"

"He says he's all right."

Jackson looked up. "But you don't buy that."

"He had to take the nitro pills during the night. I heard him get up and went to check on him."

"Made him mad, too, didn't you?"

The man read her granddad well, and Granddad grew more lavish in his praise of the hired hand all the time. They'd traded war stories and Jackson often asked for Granddad's advice, making the invalid feel needed.

"Let's say he wasn't too pleased. He's been trying to hide the episodes from me, but I counted the pills."

"What do you suppose is causing them?"

"Me."

"You?" Jackson smoothed his hands over the horse's ears and down the side of the long, arched neck. "How so?"

She gave a self-deprecating laugh. "Don't laugh now, but Granddad has this obsession. He thinks I need to get married, and until I do he won't stop fretting. He bugs me about "finding the right man" day and night, nagging that he's going to die and I'll be left all alone."

"Do you really think his condition is that bad?"

She shrugged, her hands stilling on the colt's warm back. "I hope not, but how can we really know for sure? As long as he stresses and frets over me, his blood pressure won't go down, and he'll keep having these episodes of chest pain."

"Scares you, doesn't it?"

They were inches apart, across the body of the small colt, one on each side, directly facing one another. Shannon saw the compassion in Jackson's eyes and found comfort in the kindness.

"If his health didn't scare me, I might see the humor in the whole idea of him trying to fob me off on some poor unsuspecting man. He actually thinks that's the best thing for me."

"Guess you'll have to get married then."

Shannon jerked her head up, saw he was joking and laughed. But the humor was fleeting.

"I feel so guilty knowing I'm the cause of his illness. If he should…" She couldn't bring herself to address the idea that her grandfather could actually die. "If something should happen to him I don't think I could stand it."

"Maybe you should date more. That might appease him for a while."

"Yeah," she said, voice tinged with sarcasm. "Like you see men lined up at the gate waiting to take me out."

"A woman like you can't have trouble getting a date."

"Jackson, I've dated, been engaged to and run off every decent man I know. Either they've given up, or I've lost my charm."

Did that sound as pathetic as she imagined? Sheesh. She hoped not. The one thing she didn't want was pity from Jackson.

"Sounds like you've been dating boys instead of men."

"What on earth is that supposed to mean?"

"It means if a man wants a woman bad enough, she can't run him off."

Ouch. That hurt. She'd run off all of her former loves, including Jackson.

"Which doesn't say much for my appeal then, does it, considering no one has stuck around to fight for me."

"Which proves they were a bunch of snot-nose boys, because there's definitely nothing wrong with your—" his gaze drifted up and over her "—appeal."

A skitter of excitement danced in the air between them. Shannon swallowed hard, and Jackson followed the movement, his eyes on her throat and then on her face. Heat, having nothing to do with embarrassment or the weather, flushed her skin.

She patted awkwardly at her chest. "My, it's getting hot in here."

Dumb, Shannon. Dumb.

His nostrils flared. "Sure is."

He let the colt's head ease gently to the ground. Then he stood and came around to where Shannon knelt, reached down a hand and pulled her up. Mischief in his eyes sent out a warning flare.

"What are you doing?" Her voice was raspy.

He backed her away from the horses, toward the stall door. "Demonstrating."

"But the colt," she protested, not sure she wanted to go wherever Jackson was leading.

"We'll work him again later." Jackson kept his gaze on her face, studying her as if the instructions for his puzzling behavior were written in secret code on her skin.

One minute she was backing toward the door and the next she was pressed against the hard wood with Jackson's powerful body holding her there. He slid a hand up over her throat, pressed two fingers into that spot above her collarbone where her pulse rattled like marbles in a tin can.

He was impossibly, wonderfully near, and every cell in her body remembered him. The heat and scent of him mixed with the barn scents of horse flesh and hay.

"Jacks—"

"Sshh." He laid a finger across her lips as his face came ever nearer. "Hush. Just hush."

Okay, so he was going to kiss her. And she thought she'd die of suspense waiting for him to get on with it. Instead, he stood there and stared at her, so close they were joined everywhere but the lips. She was vanilla ice cream to his hot fudge, ready to melt and mingle into a sweet, delicious pile.

He moved his fingers over her mouth, around her lips, down her throat to the edge of her tank top.

"Are you going to kiss me or not?" she demanded.

"Tsk. Tsk. So impatient." His warm, candy-scented breath whispered against her lips.

"Devil." She grabbed his face with both hands and kissed him.

A jolt of laughter rumbled from his chest into hers. He pulled back. "I'm doing the demonstrating here."

"Then get on with it."

He laughed again. Then that sexy Cajun mouth covered hers, and she went temporarily blind.

"What was that all about?" she asked when she could breathe again.

"They call it kissing."

She punched him in the chest. "Why?"

"Why do they call it kissing? I don't know. Guess we could look it up on the Internet."

"Ha-ha. Not funny. Why did you kiss me?"

His black eyes danced with orneriness. "You kissed me first, remember?"

Leave it to Jackson to bring that up. "But you started it."

He shrugged. "You were worried about losing your charms. I thought I'd check them out for you." As if totally unaffected by what had just occurred, he nonchalantly unlocked the stall door and pushed it open. A stream of sunlight filled the entry.

"And?" Was she totally pathetic or what? Begging the man to pay her a compliment.

His dimple deepened. "You want to go over to the club tonight? Free dance lessons on Tuesday."

She blinked at him, baffled. Jackson had always been like this though, so what had she expected? He could tease and please, but he never let his true feelings come to the surface. If she was looking for someone to soothe her ego, Jackson was the wrong man to ask.

* * *

When Jackson entered the ranch office that afternoon, he was still thinking about what had happened in the barn. He hadn't intended to kiss Shannon, but she'd seemed so uncharacteristically uncertain about her ability to interest a man that he'd been unable to resist. He felt sorry for her. Not that he didn't use any excuse at any time to kiss a good-looking woman, but he was here on business, not pleasure. And kissing Shannon again had certainly been all pleasure.

But he refused to regret the action. He liked her, always had, and looked forward to an evening of scooting a boot with her out at the club. They'd always had fun together, and she knew him well enough to know he wasn't interested in anything but fun and games.

"You wanted to see me, sir?"

Gus lay back in a brown leather recliner, sock feet sticking in the air. Only Gus Wyoming would insist on moving his recliner into the ranch office. But the room had his stamp all over it, from the mounted bass hanging over the huge fireplace to the old saddle piled in one corner.

Gus popped the chair lever and sat up. "Yep. Sure did. How's your aunt Bonnie getting along these days?"

"Ornery as ever." He didn't add that she was worried sick over her back mortgage payments, and he was going out of his mind trying to find a way to take care of the problem. If he'd lived a normal life, held a decent job he could borrow the money himself, but he had nothing to impress a banker.

"Yep. That's Bonnie. She and Fergus were quite a match." Gus rubbed a hand over his chest. "Too bad about Fergus. He was a good man."

"Aunt Bonnie would never have come to Texas for anybody else."

Gus gave a wheezy laugh. "I remember that. She followed him home from his trip to New Orleans. And he was smart enough not to let her leave."

Fergus had been good to Jackson's aunt in life. If only he'd planned better in case of his death.

Fretting did little good, so Jackson let the subject drop and waited for Gus to get to the point of his summons.

The older man craned his head toward the outside door. His left hand made absent, circular motions on his chest. "Shannon didn't come up with you, did she?"

Jackson blinked. What kind of question was that? "No, sir. She went to the vet's to pick up some more medication for Pat Wilson's mare."

"Good. We've got time then."

Easing down into the overstuffed chair opposite Gus, Jackson frowned. What could Gus possibly have to say to the hired man that he didn't want his granddaughter to know?

"When you planning on starting them clinics of yours to teach folks the right way to handle their horses?"

"Don't know, sir. As soon as I can."

"Money the issue?"

Talking money made Jackson anxious. "Partly. Well, mostly. It takes money to advertise and to buy or rent a good training facility." Not to mention the fact that he was spending every penny trying to bail Aunt Bonnie out of foreclosure, but he couldn't tell Gus that. His great-aunt was a private person and her money woes were his problem, not Gus's.

"I could let you use my ranch if you wanted," Gus said. "Fact of the business, I was thinking of making a deal with you."

So now the old man was getting down to the real reason behind this meeting. "A deal?"

"What do you think of my granddaughter?"

Jackson froze. Whoa. Where did that come from? He frowned. "Shannon's a...great girl."

"You think she's pretty?"

"Only a blind man wouldn't see that."

Gus liked the answer. He guffawed. "You got that right, Kane." He leaned forward. "Tell you what. I've been thinking. What with my health being bad and all, I could go at any time. I got this big old ranch and that one little granddaughter. Ain't right for her to be stuck out here alone with only a bunch of migrating ranch hands to help run this place. A woman needs a good, dependable man."

Jackson shifted uncomfortably. What happened to their horse-training discussion? "Shannon's a good trainer, old-fashioned and hard-headed maybe, but she can handle this ranch and every horse on it."

"Glad you see that because my Shannon won't kowtow to any man, husband or not."

"I'm afraid I've lost the thread of this discussion." At least he hoped he'd lost the thread. He didn't even want to consider that Gus was suggesting a marriage between him and Shannon. A shudder of horror ran through him. Sweat popped out on the back of his neck. Marriage. No way.

"Ah, heck, I ain't doing this right. Here's the deal, straight out. I like you, Kane. You're a good man. If you'll marry my granddaughter, I'll not only sponsor your clinics and let you have them right here, I'll give you a part interest in this ranch—providing you do right by Shannon, that is."

If the room had been full of flies, Jackson would have caught them all in his open mouth. Two full minutes went by while outside horses whinnied and a truck motor roared. Shannon was back, a sure sign that he had better finish this conversation fast.

"I don't know what to say."

"Say you'll think about it. You'll have what you want now instead of having to wait two or three years to get it. And I'll have the peace of mind knowing Shannon has someone to look after her."

"Do you know how furious she'd be if she knew about this?"

Gus's face showed alarm. He leaned back, patting his chest. "You won't tell her?"

He wanted to. They'd both be better off to get this thing out in the open, to be honest with Shannon, but she'd be hurt by her granddad's maneuverings. Oh, she'd act mad, but she'd be humiliated, and Jackson didn't want that.

"Promise me, boy. Promise me. Shannon can't ever know about this." The old man slapped at his shirt pocket, pulling out a pill bottle. With trembling hands, he shook out a tiny white tablet and stuck the medication under his tongue.

Jackson shoved out of his chair so fast his hat fell to the floor with a soft thud. He rushed to Gus's side, helpless to know what else to do but make a promise he'd probably regret.

"Okay, Gus. Take it easy. You have my word. I won't tell Shannon a thing about this."

"And you'll think about my proposition?"

"Sure. Sure. I'll think about it."

The old man had just offered him the dream he'd been pursuing for years with the added bonus of a partial interest in a fine training facility. The money he needed to help his aunt was dangling right in front of him. There was only one catch. Marry the owner's granddaughter to get it.

How could he think about anything else?

Chapter Four

The ride into Rattlesnake that evening took less than ten minutes. To Shannon, who was still thinking about that morning's killer kiss, sitting next to Jackson for even ten minutes did funny things to her head. She hadn't quite decided if she'd agreed to this date because she wanted to go dancing or because she needed to prove that Jackson Kane's kiss didn't mean a thing.

They'd just reached the outskirts of town when Jackson turned his dark gaze her way. "Mind if we wheel by Aunt Bonnie's first?"

"Not at all. I'd love to say hello to your aunt." And that was the truth. Talking to the feisty lady would get her mind off Jackson's mouth. The constant movement of the tiny sucker between his lips was disconcerting.

"Your teeth are going to rot," she said, partly out of self-defense and partly to annoy Jackson.

A smile perfect enough for a toothpaste ad gleamed at her. "Better to lose my teeth than my life."

"Gee, I didn't know those little suckers were such powerful medicine," she quipped, knowing full well what he meant. Too many country boys started using smokeless tobacco in their teens and then found themselves too hooked to stop.

"Better than dipping. Gave it up a while back, but I can't seem to give up the Dum-Dums. Maybe I'll work my way into sugarless someday." He tossed one to her. "Join me."

"How evil of you." She grinned and unwrapped the grape candy. "Wickedness always wants to take someone down with it."

"If I sweeten you up enough, maybe you'll come to your senses and let me teach you the proper way to train a horse."

He had the goofiest ideas. Imagine caring what a horse was thinking about. Sheesh. Like it mattered. A horse was an animal, not a kid.

"In your dreams, Kane."

With a mischievous twitch of his eyebrows, he wheeled into the concrete driveway of a modest brick house in one of the older neighborhoods in Rattlesnake. Neat pots of colorful plants lined the concrete porch and well-tended flower beds edged the front of the house. Hummingbird feeders hanging from either end of the porch were swarmed by the tiny iridescent-green birds.

A pair of metal rocking chairs sat empty under a huge live oak.

"She's probably around back in the garden," Jackson said. "That woman never stays in the house."

He led the way to the back where, sure enough, Bonnie was working in her garden, back bent in two as she picked cucumbers. She wore jersey gloves and a straw hat tied beneath her chin with a floral scarf. She was tiny, probably didn't weigh ninety pounds soaking wet and her skin, dark like Jackson's, was wrinkled with time and character.

At their approach, she straightened. Her black eyes snapped with intelligence and lively humor. "Well, look here what the wind blew in."

"Hello, Miss Bonnie," Shannon said. "How have you been?"

"Fine. Fine." The little woman swiped a hand over her moist brow. "How did your blackened fish turn out?"

"Not as good as yours, I'm sure, but passable. Granddad ate it anyway." By way of explanation, she said to Jackson, "The last time I was in the grocery store your aunt gave me her recipe."

"She's a great cook."

"Oh, go on with you, boy," Bonnie said. "You only say that so I'll keep feeding you."

Jackson favored her with an affectionate grin. "Dang right."

"Here now. Quit your cussing." She glanced at Shannon in resignation. "I raised him better than that.

Guess I'll have to wash his mouth out with soap again."

Jackson groaned and shook his head.

Shannon could hardly keep a straight face. The thought of this tiny flea of a woman correcting her big ornery nephew was too funny. "Are you telling me I should watch out for him?"

Bonnie's dark eyes danced with mischief. Shannon could see where Jackson had gotten his propensity for teasing.

"Oh, absolutely, honey. A girl can't be too careful of the company she keeps."

"Hey," Jackson said, pretending insult. "No fair ganging up on the only male."

"All right. We'll let you off the hook if you'll get that bushel basket off the porch for me. I want to get these cucumbers picked before dark."

"Why not pick them in the morning, Auntie B., when it's cooler? Better yet, leave them for me."

"Now don't start. You know I love my garden," Bonnie said, waving off his concern with a gloved hand as she turned to Shannon. "He's such a fuss-budget." But there was affection and pleasure in the statement.

"Just returning the favor. You did the same to me when I was a boy."

"Be that as it may, young man, I can't pick these to-morrow. I'm headed over to the old folks' home first thing in the morning to help out with breakfast. Then

I'm off to work at ten. But if I can put these cukes in the lime bath tonight, I can finish the pickling in time to take a few jars to the church supper. Preacher's mighty fond of my sweet pickles."

"You do too much."

"I love doing for others. That's how I get my blessings."

Jackson's brows drew together in a frown. "If you'd quit that job, you'd have time for the things you enjoy instead of standing on your feet all day behind a cash register."

Smiling softly, Bonnie patted his cheek. "Can't, darlin' boy. And you know it."

With a fierce expression, Jackson gripped the wrinkled brown fingers and held them against his face. "Not yet, but you will. I promise."

The little woman was well past retirement age, but she had worked full-time as a grocery clerk since her husband's death. An older person working wasn't so unusual, but Jackson's reaction was. He hadn't been around Rattlesnake for nearly ten years so why should he suddenly be so protective of his elderly aunt?

Rather than spy on what must be an ongoing family argument, Shannon began searching through the heavy vines, pulling cucumbers.

"You don't have to do that, honey," Bonnie said as she returned to her work.

"I don't mind." Shannon tossed a couple of the fat vegetables into the bucket and motioned to Jackson. "Be useful, Cajun boy."

With an exasperated shake of his head, Jackson bent to the job. After a minute, he grumbled, "There's a bumblebee in here."

Shannon slapped a gnat on her arm. "Bonnie's sweet pickles are worth the risk."

"Easy for you to say. I'm the one looking at the business end of a killer bee."

"He's after the sugar. Just offer him a Dum-Dum and keep working."

Shannon no more than got the smart-aleck words out of her mouth than Jackson jerked upright, let out a howl and clutched his fingertips.

Great, the big goof must have gotten himself stung. Guilt-stricken, Shannon rushed to his side and grabbed his hand, hardly noticing that Bonnie watched, grinning like a possum. "Did he sting you?"

"No." Onyx eyes laughed down at her. "I just wanted to see if you would hold my hand."

She dropped it like a red-hot branding iron. "Oh, you!"

Jackson laughed and turned to his aunt. "I think we got 'em all."

"I think you got Shannon instead, you ornery snake." They exchanged smiles. "Good enough for now. Especially since you riled up that bumblebee with your howling and thrashing." Bonnie dusted her hands together and drew off the gloves.

With his usual swagger, Jackson hefted the filled bucket and they went into the house through the back door.

Shannon liked Bonnie Watley's kitchen. Light, airy

and mostly white with splashes of blue here and there, it was as tidy as the woman's gardens and as welcoming as her smile.

"Where do you want these, Auntie B.?" Jackson asked.

"The sink will do. I'll wash and slice them later." She peeled the hat from her head and tossed it onto a chair. "Do you kids want something to eat or drink?"

"No thanks. We're headed over to Cowboys. We'll have something there." Jackson dumped the cucumbers into the spotless sink and ran the sprayer over them. "Anything else we can do before we leave?"

"No, you two go on."

"I may be late."

"You're a grown man. I don't keep tabs on you."

"Sure you do." He smooched his aunt on the cheek. "You'll be okay?"

"Been by myself for three years, son. I'll be fine."

"I know, but…"

"No buts. Go on now. You're making me feel old." She shooed him. "Shannon, tell that grandpop of yours hello. When he gets to feeling better, I want the two of you to come for supper."

"Why, Miss Bonnie, that would be wonderful. I'll tell him."

"Good." She patted Jackson's chest. "Behave yourself now."

Jackson aimed a wicked dimple at Shannon and said, "Impossible, Auntie. Impossible."

* * *

Smoke swirled around Shannon's head as she pre-ceded Jackson into Cowboys, a local country-western watering hole and dance floor. Jackson's hand rested lightly, but disturbingly, at the small of her back. She was quite capable of walking into a club on her own, thank you. The fact that he'd been as sweet as one of his suckers to his aunt and had seemed genuinely con-cerned for the lady's welfare gave Shannon enough fits without him touching her. The apparent change in him from reckless cowboy to responsible nephew made keeping an emotional distance that much harder.

A rowdy honky-tonk tune blasted from the jukebox as they entered. A half-dozen heads swiveled, hands lifted and voices called out hellos. In a town this small, Shannon knew everyone, at least by name or reputation.

"Want some nachos?" Jackson shouted close to her ear.

"A Coke will do."

Round tables were scattered along the edge of the dance floor. She made her way to one of these, stopping once to exchange pleasantries with a young man who'd helped out on the ranch last summer. She felt out of place, as though she were too old to be here. Shrugging off the notion, she settled into a chair and watched Jackson maneuver through the dancers like a running back through a line of tacklers.

He slid the cola in front of her and scraped up a chair. "Ready for that dance lesson?"

"Let me drink my Coke first." She took a sip, letting the chill slide soothingly down her throat. "First, I want to discuss Ginger."

Earlier that day, they'd argued about the mare. Shannon was certain the horse only needed a firm hand to break her from balking at water crossings.

The jukebox kicked into a slow, quieter waltz that made talking much easier. Jackson folded his hands on the table and leaned forward. "We have to convince Ginger that the water is not her enemy. Horses have brains, Shannon. They can think."

It was an old argument. "Humans are the dominant species. It's up to us to take control and show an animal who is in charge."

"So," he said with a maddening smile. "When is Domino going to figure that out?"

"Soon." She ignored the jab. Domino was nowhere near ready to return to his owners and the problem was wearing on Shannon's confidence. If she weren't so stubborn and if Jackson were anyone else, she would ask his advice. "I watched you in the round pen today."

"I know."

His reply surprised her. He'd been so intent on the bay gelding running circles around the pen, Shannon had assumed he'd been oblivious to her presence.

Another loud song replaced the waltz. Jackson leaned closer. Shannon tried not to look at the supple movement of his lips or the way the tiny laugh lines danced around his eyes. "What did you think?"

Pretending to watch the dancers, she toyed with her glass. She knew he was asking about his ability as a trainer, and though she was impressed, she wouldn't give him the satisfaction of knowing it. She'd been watching him off and on for a month, and there was no doubt he had an uncanny way with horses.

She looked up, and then wished she hadn't. In the cramped and noisy club, he was, of necessity, impossibly near. Her pulse jerked in a totally inappropriate manner. "I thought he looked worried."

"That was the point. I was playing the herd mare—" His dimple flared and so did a tiny fire in her belly. Darn it. "I had him exiled from the herd by my actions. But did you notice how he came docily to me when I relaxed my stance and stopped staring at him?"

"Is that how it works with you horse-psychologist types?" she said, voice laced with sarcasm. "You play horsey?"

Not taking the bait, Jackson continued to explain as patiently as though she were one of his headstrong mares. The notion annoyed her even more.

"Learning the horse's signals, knowing how he thinks and understanding his herd mentality gives me the advantage over him."

Shannon shook her head. Psychology for a horse. Ridiculous. Next he'd be telling her that horses fell in love with each other. "Sorry, I just don't get it."

"Your grandfather does."

"Is that what the two of you were talking about when I came in from the vet's this afternoon?" She swiveled the ice in her glass. "Conspiring behind my back?"

She was only joking, but the guilty expression on

Jackson's face made her suspicious. If he was trying to persuade her granddad to let him take over as head trainer, she had a right to know.

Jackson saw the danger signals as soon as Shannon's blue eyes narrowed. She was a smart woman. If she started asking questions before he was ready to answer, he'd make a mess of things, probably blunder around and tell her about Gus's crazy offer. She and Gus would both be furious, and he'd be out of the job he desperately needed.

"Come on, lady." He grabbed her hand and pulled. "We came to dance."

Though Shannon's expression said she wasn't fooled, she followed him on to the floor. Her pale blond hair brushed the tips of her bare shoulders and gleamed in the flickering lights as she began to move to the music.

On a small portable stage at one end of the rectangular floor, a middle-aged redhead in snug jeans and fringed shirt demonstrated simple dance steps. A few couples watched and imitated, but most, like Jackson and Shannon, favored the old familiar dances.

Sliding easily into a two-step, Jackson held Shannon at a comfortable distance. She was already riled up. No use pulling her as close as he wanted to. She looked hotter than fresh coffee in a pair of snug jeans with lace down the legs. Lace, for Pete's sake, a reminder that, rancher though she may be, Shannon Wyoming was female to the bone.

When the music slowed to another waltz, Shannon started to pull away. For reasons he would later question, Jackson drew her back to him. She stiffened for a moment, but when he challenged with a look, her chin shot up and she leaned into him.

The second her body aligned with his, Jackson's brain threatened to short-circuit. Just like this morning when he'd kissed her, his breath clogged in his chest. Man, she smelled good. And for a woman who worked outside in the sun, her skin was softer than a feather pillow.

Her breath brushed his ear and he suppressed a shiver. Gus and his unthinkable ideas had Jackson's mind going in a direction he'd never intended.

"Jackson." Shannon's silky voice had him thinking of clean sheets.

"Yeah?" Where had the gravel in his throat come from?

"What were you and Granddad talking about?"

His libido crashed and burned. So much for thinking she was hot for him. Sneaky witch. He should have known she wouldn't drop the subject of his discussion with Gus. But at least he'd had time to come up with a plausible answer.

He lifted his shoulders in a nonchalant shrug as if the conversation with her grandfather hadn't rocked his world. "He's worried about you. Thinks you're too stubborn to get married, and he'll die and leave you all alone."

"Not again." She closed her eyes and laid her forehead against his chest. Cool. He could deal with that.

"You do realize, don't you, that my grandfather had an ulterior motive for bringing you into this obsession of his?" She looked up at him, all blue eyes and frustration.

Keeping his face as innocent as possible while wishing she'd kept her pretty little head right where it was, Jackson replied, "What kind of motive?"

If she had an inkling of Gus's offer, she'd throw a fit to rival a nuclear explosion.

"He's trying to push us together." Shannon didn't blush too often, but a hint of color bloomed on her cheeks. "He thinks you are fine husband material. You're a great horseman and according to Granddad—" she paused dramatically "—you're clean."

"Clean?"

They both laughed. Some of the tension left him. "Come on, let's sit down. This conversation is getting squirrelly."

Still holding her hand and liking the way it felt inside his, Jackson led the way back to the table.

Shannon lifted her hair on each side and let it fall, her gaze focused somewhere across the room. A pretty frown drew her eyebrows together.

"You know," she said, "I've been giving this some thought. Maybe I could hire somebody."

She'd lost him. "To do what?"

"Marry me." At the shock that must have registered on his face, she flapped one hand at him. "Oh, not for real and forever. But maybe I could hire some nincompoop to pretend to be my husband temporarily. You know, a make-believe thing. Just until Granddad gets back on his feet."

"And what would you do with the nincompoop after Gus is up and going again?"

"I don't know. Run him off, I guess, and tell Granddad it just didn't work out. I'm an expert at getting rid of men." She blew out a breath. "And I sure don't want or need a husband."

"I know exactly what you mean." He gave a mock shudder. "But I don't think you'll find any man willing to play along with that kind of game. First of all, he really would have to be a nincompoop—and Gus would never fall for that. He knows you too well."

"That's true. And to be honest, there aren't any men left in Rattlesnake who would give me the time of day, much less marry me. I've pretty much run out of interested prospects." Shoulders drooping, she slid down in her chair and gnawed on the side of her thumbnail.

There was that uncertainty, that vulnerability again.

Jackson shifted on the hard wooden chair. A germ of an idea pushed at his brain. He tried to shake it off. Bad idea. A very bad idea.

"Oh, come on, Shan. There has to be somebody. You're not exactly hard to look at."

"Why, thanks, Kane. I think that was almost a compliment."

Jackson had to bite his tongue to keep from telling her how beautiful and sexy she was. In the years since they'd last been together, something had worn away at her confidence. She probably wouldn't believe him anyway.

Marry her, Kane.

The idea was back. Less threatening now for some unexplainable reason.

Gus's voice, like a broken record in his head, urged him to marry Shannon. Earlier the idea had scared him sideways. But now, with Shannon sitting across the table, her eyes vulnerable and uncertain, the notion held a certain appeal. A temporary arrangement didn't sound so bad, just until Gus was better and until the training symposia were up and running. He'd be doing the old man a favor, helping him regain his health. Who better than he, a man who had no intention of ever being a real husband, to agree to a short-term marriage of convenience? Maybe Gus was right. Maybe he was the perfect candidate. Shannon would be relieved knowing she had made her grandfather happy. On the other hand, she'd be furious if she discovered the deal Gus had offered him.

Stewing on that one troubling detail, Jackson leaned back in his chair and pretended to watch the couples cruising across the dance floor. The deal would have to remain a secret between him and Gus. Total secrecy was the only way this would work. Shannon couldn't ever know what her grandfather had promised him in exchange for the marriage.

Best of all, his career would be off to a roaring start, and he could earn the money Aunt Bonnie needed much more quickly.

His own thought processes startled him. Was he actually considering Gus's suggestion?

Yeah. He was.

What the heck? It was a win-win situation. Everyone got what they wanted.

Convinced he was doing the right thing and that his motives were pure, he leaned forward and reclaimed Shannon's hand. Her skin was cool from the Coke glass. And soft. It was real soft.

"What if I could find a husband for you, a man who would agree to a marriage—short-term, of course— while Gus gets back on his feet."

Her blue eyes widened. "Are you serious?"

He swallowed. Was he? "Yeah."

"Who?"

His heart gave one painful thump right before he jumped off the cliff. "Me."

Chapter Five

Shannon jumped up and was out the door in a time that would have pleased Carl Lewis. She needed air. She needed a clear head. And what she didn't need was the black-eyed Cajun following her.

"Gee, Shannon," Jackson said as he caught up to where she leaned on the hood of his truck gasping for air. "You sure know how to make a guy feel good about his proposal."

"That wasn't a proposal, that was a—" She gulped past the confusion in her throat. "What was it?"

"I was offering you a way out of your dilemma." As if they were discussing a ride on a merry-go-round, Jackson's dimples flashed in the dim lights of the parking area.

Memories of ten years ago flooded through her. Hands shaking, she hugged herself, rubbing suddenly chilled arms. "Why? Why would you even consider such a thing?"

Her heart was racing wildly, but Jackson sounded as calm as a morning pond. "Why not? I'm unattached and plan to stay that way. I like your grandfather. And I'm at the ranch every day anyway."

"What's in it for you?"

"Ah, now that's the interesting thing." He moved close and rubbed calloused hands over her arms. His touch did not help matters in the least. "There's this woman, see?"

She might have known. She tried to yank away from him, but he refused to let her go.

"And she's been pressuring me about marriage, babies, the whole enchilada." His hands had worked their way up to her neck. He lifted her hair, sifted it through his hands. "A wedding between you and me would put an end to that."

Jealousy, unwelcome and irritating, pinched at Shannon. She kept her arms firmly folded, refusing to enjoy his delicious touch. Men. They were all jerks.

"Just for that—" she glared at him, not wanting to miss the shock on his face "—I accept."

But Jackson surprised her. He didn't look shocked at all. He waited one beat, then stepped back and stuck out his hand. "Deal."

Holy moly, she thought, as she placed her hand in his. She had just agreed to get married—to the only man who'd ever broken her heart.

Had she completely lost her mind?

* * *

Hairbrush in hand, Shannon stared into the full-length mirror at the panic in her eyes and the pallor of her skin.

"Can you say terrified?" she muttered to the ghastly reflection.

She was still struggling to believe she and Jackson had finally agreed on something. And that something was a temporary marriage. Today was their wedding day, if you could call this impromptu gathering a wedding.

After she had found her voice that night at the club and had stopped shaking, they'd hashed out the details on the way back to the ranch.

She might not trust Jackson in a lot of things, but she could trust him on this. He would walk away when the time was right—whenever that might be—no harm, no foul. The charming Cajun no more wanted to be married than she did.

At first she'd battled a healthy dose of guilt over deceiving her grandfather. But during the two weeks since they'd announced the engagement, Gus had been so much happier and more energetic. His renewed vigor was proof enough that she'd found the best solution under the circumstances.

She wished things could be different. She wished she was marrying for the right reasons, but she'd blown all those chances long ago.

Shrugging off the faint depression that had settled over her the minute she'd gotten out of bed this morn-

10204518

TAKE

$10.00 OFF*

your next BON•TON
credit card purchase
of $50.00 or more

*See back for details.

ing, Shannon ran the brush through her hair for the third time and checked her appearance in the mirror.

She would have preferred jeans, but she and Jackson had agreed to play the part and do nothing to raise Granddad's suspicions. So she'd opted for her favorite long embroidered skirt. The off-white mesh material and scalloped hem made her feel feminine, though she didn't know why she cared. She'd added a lace tank top, then finished the outfit off with a short jean jacket, a wide low-rider belt and a pair of snazzy sandals.

Satisfied that her appearance would pass, she ran damp palms over her skirt and went downstairs to the living room—and her temporary groom.

But only Gus waited there. Looking smug and pleased, his cheeks slick and shiny from an extra-close shave, he stood in front of the empty fireplace. Over the mantel hung a family portrait, the only one ever taken of her mother, father and the two-year-old child she'd once been. Here, in front of family, both dead and alive, was where the vows would be exchanged.

Shannon tried not to think about that part.

"There's the bride." Gus's smile stretched from ear to ear. "Come here, baby girl." He opened his arms. "This is the happiest day of my life."

Shannon's heart swelled with love as she walked into Gus's hug. She was doing the right thing by marrying Jackson for the sake of Granddad's health. Soon, his blood pressure and stress would be under control, and he could be outside again doing what he loved best. Giving him back his life was worth any sacrifice.

And what then? a voice nagged. What would the inevitable breakup do to Gus's health? Neither she nor Jackson had thought that far ahead. For now, she pushed the worry away. Today she could make her grandfather happy. She would figure out the rest when the time came.

Dual engines roared into the driveway. Shannon's nerves, already jumping, formed a knot at the base of her skull. She straightened her belt, pasted on a fake smile and opened the door to the only wedding guests, Jett and Becka Garret. Jett had been Jackson's friend and traveling partner until an injury had sidelined the wildest Garret. Becka, Shannon's closest friend, had been his nurse. No one had been more surprised than Shannon when the two had fallen madly in love and married.

Becka, looking petite and pretty in a coral sundress, offered a quick hug and whispered, "Are you sure about this?"

Not at all certain, but very determined, Shannon responded with a nod of her head, then showed her friends inside. Besides Jackson, Becka was the only other person who knew the real story behind this charade of a wedding. Over the years, the friends had shared many secrets, including the most painful one of all. No doubt that ten-year-old memory prompted Becka's deep concern.

Behind the Garrets came the remaining members of

the wedding party: Jackson, his aunt and the justice of the peace.

A slow, admiring smile spread over Jackson's darkly handsome face when his eyes met Shannon's. "Looking good, Miss Wyoming." He handed her a bouquet of daisies and kissed her cheek.

The manly combination of his woodsy fragrance and warm lips sent her senses reeling, but it was the flowers that almost did her in. She had wanted no fuss, no bother. Just do what had to be done. But the flowers made the wedding real—and personal. Was it a fluke or had he remembered that she loved daisies?

Her smile trembled. "Ready?"

"Settin' on go." He looked so handsome and at ease, Shannon had to fight the quiver of attraction that ran though her belly.

Clutching the bouquet to her waist, she took her place beside him in front of the fireplace. Gus and Bonnie settled in on either side with the justice of the peace in front. The Garrets took a seat on the sofa. Jett looked amused. Becka worried her bottom lip. Bonnie kept dabbing at her eyes with a tissue. And Granddad beamed as the ceremony began.

Just as she couldn't remember the dead parents smiling down at her, Shannon never could recall the next few minutes of her life. She felt Jackson beside her, heard him clear his throat a couple of times, and knew she must have spoken the appropriate words. But the roaring in her head didn't stop until Jackson touched her shoulders and pulled her toward him. As soon as his mouth closed over hers, reality struck. She had done it. She was married—however temporarily—to Jackson Kane.

"Oh, honey, that was so sweet." Bonnie grabbed them both in a group hug. "Didn't you think so, Gus?"

Gus took his turn for a hug and kiss, happiness glowing on him like fireplace embers. He shook hands with Jackson and clapped him on the back. "Welcome to the family, son."

Jackson, who'd lost his nonchalance during the ceremony, looked no less shell-shocked than she felt. But given Gus's reaction, she believed with all her heart the marriage was the right decision.

"This calls for a celebration," Bonnie said. "Gus, did you order cake?"

Gus looked crestfallen. "I never thought about cake."

"That's okay, Granddad." Shannon didn't want anything to spoil his happiness. "We don't care about cake."

Becka came up beside them and said, "I wish we'd thought about it. Cookie would have loved making a wedding cake."

"No cake, no punch." Bonnie fretted. "We gotta celebrate with something."

With both Jackson and Shannon protesting, the two elders worried over their lack of planning. Finally, Bonnie brightened.

"Well, it may not be as fancy as cake, but I brought y'all some sweet pickles."

The entire party froze and then burst out laughing.

So in the end, they spent an hour around the kitchen table, listening to Bonnie and Gus tell childhood stories about the bride and groom while they ate a jar of Bonnie's best sweet pickles and drank iced tea.

The wedding night was not quite so simple.

Jackson rubbed the knot on the back of his neck and gazed around Shannon's bedroom. Lavender and white was a little too girlie for him, but he could live with it for now. He spent most of his time outside anyway. And when he was in here, the lights would usually be out, Shannon would be in his arms, and he wouldn't be thinking about lavender chiffon at all.

His bride—the word had a surprisingly sweet ring to it—swept the fringed belt from her skirt and tossed it over a chair. Jackson's fatigue evaporated. If Shannon planned to undress in front of him, he was ready for the show. Fact was, he'd thought of little else since she'd agreed to this marriage charade.

"Well," she said. "We did it, didn't we?"

"Not yet, but I was planning to as soon as you take off that skirt." Weddings weren't good. Wedding nights were awesome.

Shannon gave him a you're-a-dead-man-if-you-think-that look. "We are not going to do *it,* Jackson. I thought you were clear on that."

Disappointment hit him below the belt. He fumbled in his shirt pocket for a sucker. "Why not?"

She slapped a hand on her hip. "Hello! This is not a

real marriage. We didn't even have a cake. There will be no wedding night."

"I can buy you a cake."

She threw a pillow at him.

He laughed. "Okay. Forget the cake."

"If not for raising Granddad's suspicions, I wouldn't even be sharing a room with you."

"We're married, Shan. Might as well enjoy *it*."

"No." She opened the oversize chest of drawers and took out a gauzy nightgown. "That would only complicate matters."

He closed the space between them, took her upper arms and tried to pull her close. "It's not like we haven't before."

Stiffening, her face going rigid, Shannon's eyes flashed something that he would swear was pain. "No, Jackson."

Puzzled, he let her push past him and go into the bathroom.

Sitting down on the bed, he pulled off his shoes and unbuttoned his shirt. What was that all about? They were married. Married people did...*it*.

He flopped backward onto the bed and folded his arms behind his head, thinking. Everything would come together sooner or later. Shannon was a passionate woman. She'd come around eventually if he could be patient. Horse training took enormous patience. He knew how to bide his time.

She came out of the bathroom, wearing the calf-length blue nightgown that wasn't intended to be sexy, but his body temperature went up ten degrees. The material wasn't see-through, but it molded to her body in tantalizing ways when she moved.

He gritted his teeth. So much for patience.

Shannon fumbled with the string tie at the neck of her gown. Ever since she and Jackson had agreed on this make-believe marriage, she had wondered what this night would be like. There was no way she could sleep with him. The consequences of that game were too dire, and she refused to suffer through that again.

And yet, there lay her husband—the man she'd once cried over and prayed would come back to her—with his shirt unbuttoned and his well-muscled, beautifully browned chest much more masculine that it had been ten years ago. His washboard belly would make any woman drool. And heaven only knew what the rest of him looked like.

"Tell me you brought pajamas," she blurted.

Sexy dimples flared. "Real men don't wear pajamas."

"I'm buying you a pair tomorrow."

"I won't wear them." He stood up and began to shuck his clothes. "You may force me to be celibate, but I don't intend to make it easy on you."

"So you think you're that hot? That irresistible?"

He tossed his shirt to her, then reached for the button on his jeans. "Do you?"

"Doing a striptease will not turn me on or change my mind."

With a smile and a shrug, he continued to undress. If she turned away, he'd think she wanted him. Refusing to give him the satisfaction, she tilted her head to one side and watched.

By the time he reached his boxers, she was praying he'd stop. His athlete's body was incredible. And she really, really wanted to touch him.

Holding her gaze, he ran a finger around the waistband. She swallowed, barely breathing.

"You're getting turned on."

"I am not." She flounced around to her side of the bed, yanked back the covers and slid under, turning her back to him. Behind her came a faint rustling, then the bed dipped and he slipped in beside her. His foot found hers.

"Don't you want to know if I'm naked?" His voice was close to her ear and full of teasing laughter.

"Doesn't matter to me," she said as breezily as she could.

He scooted closer, draped an arm over her middle. "It will. Maybe not tonight, but sooner or later it will matter."

Shannon awoke to the sound of a man singing in the shower. She drew a pillow over her head, but the darned thing smelled like Jackson so she traded it for her own.

She'd slept little, thanks to Jackson's amazing body pressing against hers all night. She'd almost turned to him once, but the painful memories of the last time wouldn't let her.

Attraction was a complication she hadn't planned for. Now wasn't that stupid, considering their history?

Squeezing her eyelids tight, she repeated a nursery rhyme and tried to forget that a very hunky Cajun was in her bathroom. She must have dozed again, because the next thing she knew the hunky Cajun was tugging the pillow from her face.

"Morning, Mrs. Kane." He handed her a cup of coffee. "Do you always look this sexy when you wake up?"

She pushed the hair out of her face and sat up, trying not to notice how impossibly handsome he looked.

"Where did you get coffee?" She took a sip and hummed her appreciation.

"The kitchen. I've been up for an hour or so. Had breakfast with Gus." He scooted her hip with his and sat down on the bed. "He's happy as a hog in a fresh mud wallow."

Shannon laughed. "He said that, didn't he?"

"Yep. Even offered to buy us a honeymoon trip, but I assured him we had too much work to do."

"Good thinking, cowboy." The last thing she could handle right now was being alone with Jackson in a secluded spot. Sitting beside him in her nightgown was problem enough. Abandoning the last of her beloved coffee, she shimmied around him and got up, making her escape.

Less than twenty-four hours into this make-believe marriage and Shannon was already in big trouble.

Chapter Six

Three weeks later Jackson unloaded an Appaloosa stallion from the air-conditioned trailer and led him into a freshly prepared stall. Eyes wide and rolling, the stallion whinnied and tried to rear. The horse had been handled improperly to Jackson's way of thinking and now required a great deal of conditioning to correct. He could do it, in time, but the animal was as unruly and difficult as the woman he'd married. He could solve the horse's problem. The wife problem had him buffaloed.

Satisfied the horse was settled enough to leave alone, Jackson backed away and ran a hand over his face. He was tired. Worn out from night after night without enough sleep. He'd even thought of sleeping on the bathroom floor, but Shannon's presence was there, too.

Sharing a room with his lovely bride was much more

difficult than he'd anticipated. The smell of her shampoo, her underwear tossed here and there, but most of all her soft body curled next to his night after night was killing him.

He worked himself into exhaustion every day, hoping to drive thoughts of her out of his head. But his efforts had all been in vain. Shannon, sassy and full of challenge, danced around the edges of his mind all the time. And every time he tried to concentrate on plans for his symposium, she'd come sashaying around a corner, making him want to grab her for a kiss. He'd done it a few times, too, and she'd been ornery enough to kiss him back. Touching her had only made things worse.

He glanced around the various corrals and pens in search of his troublesome bride. Earlier he'd watched her ride off on a skittish yearling that still needed a lot of training. She'd been gone quite a while if memory served.

A strange discomfort gripped his gut. Where was she? Had she made it back? Was she okay?

Grunting a small, disparaging sound, he kicked a dried horse patty with his boot toe and started toward the house. Shannon would laugh in his face if she knew he was fretting over her safety. But she was his wife, real or not, and a man had a certain responsibility in caring for what was his regardless of the circumstance.

The entire situation disgruntled him. Shannon was messing with his mind and his emotions in a big way, and he didn't much like it.

He hadn't yet broached the topic of putting on a

training clinic, but he had to soon. Shannon had heard Gus and him casually toss around ideas but she had no clue that they were talking in the here and now. Fall, only a couple of months away, would be the best time and such an event took planning and advertising.

The house was quiet when he entered. No surprise there. That was one reason he'd come inside. During this quiet time, he could work up some plans for the clinic.

Gus had gone to see Dr. Torrence for his checkup. From the old man's improved vitality, Jackson and Shannon both were confident the news would be good. Gus had also made noises about going by to see Bonnie to talk her out of another jar of pickles. With a shake of his head, Jackson smiled. What was *that* all about?

Tromping upstairs for a good wash, Jackson pushed the bedroom door open…and went temporarily blind.

Her back to him, Shannon stood in front of the mirror dressed in a towel. Shoulders glistening with moisture, her hair wet, she must have just gotten out of the shower.

Her eyes met his in the mirror. Most women would bolt and grab for a robe. Not Shannon. Her chin hitched upward in a challenge. This was her room, her house, and having him around didn't phase her in the least.

Oh man.

Without thinking it through, he moved toward her, watched her blue eyes widen without wavering as he touched her shoulders. The opportunity was here. He simply couldn't resist it.

Leaning down he kissed the soft curve of her shoulder, felt her shiver, and was pretty darn glad to know he had an effect on her. She certainly had one on him.

As Shannon's sweet fragrance wrapped around his senses, he lifted the damp hair and brushed his lips over her neck. During his ten years away, he'd never forgotten that sexy blend of woman and denim and flowers that was Shannon's alone.

Slowly turning her, his body tingling all over, Jackson cupped her face and wondered if the time had finally come. She responded by sliding her arms up his chest and over his shoulders. He pulled her close and kissed her. Her lips were warm and moist and sweet enough to make his teeth hurt. He loved kissing her and he was certain she felt the same. For all her denials, they couldn't keep their hands off each other.

The dampness from her towel seeped through his shirt, but did nothing to cool his simmering blood. He reached for the knotted terry cloth. Instantly, Shannon stiffened and pulled back. The challenge evaporated from her expression to be replaced by anxiety. Dang it, why should she be anxious? He was her husband.

One hand holding the towel together, she shook her head. "I'm sorry. We can't do this."

Disappointment made him gruff. "Then why did you kiss me back?"

One glistening, tempting shoulder hitched. "I like kissing."

If he hadn't been so frustrated he would have

laughed. "Yeah, so I noticed, but a man can only take so much, Shannon. You parade around half-naked, what do you expect me to think?"

She took offense to that. "I didn't know you were in the house."

He held up a hand. "But you knew I was in this room and yet you did nothing to cover up. Then you kissed me like—like—you know how you kissed me." All his frustrations rushed out in a growl. "You didn't use to be a tease."

"A tease?" She looked crestfallen. "Is that what you think? That I'm purposely leading you on so I can turn you down?"

"What else can I think?"

Stricken, she wilted away from him. "Oh, Jackson, I'm sorry. I really am. It's just that—that—"

She put a trembling hand to her mouth and Jackson suppressed the urge to hold her again. Shannon was supposed to be tough. Any hint of vulnerability really got to him.

"What?"

But she wouldn't elaborate.

"Nothing. Nothing." She went to the closet and took out a robe, slipping it on. "I just didn't expect this to be so hard."

He allowed a short, mirthless laugh. "Welcome to the club. Maybe I should find somewhere else to sleep."

She spun toward him. "You can't do that! Granddad's health is improving every day. We can't risk him knowing the truth."

What would she say if he told her that Gus already knew the truth in part because the marriage had been his idea? But then again, Gus had no idea the arrangement was anything but permanent.

Jackson backed off, shoving a hand over the top of his head. No wonder he'd always been against marriage. Look at the mess he'd gotten into with this one.

"Okay. You're right. Gus is the important one here. We'll deal with this, though the solution is already clear to me. We're married. The next step is over there in that prissy lavender bed of yours. As far as I'm concerned that would settle all this tiptoeing around each other."

She shook her head; the damp ends of her hair made soft flapping sounds against her skin. "There are some things you don't understand, Jackson."

"I would if you'd tell me."

Blue eyes flickered uncertainly before she glanced away. Something bad was eating at her, but she wasn't ready to share it with the likes of him.

Resigned for the moment, he went to his sock drawer and took out a bag of Dum-Dums.

"Truce?" he said, offering her one.

A tentative smile tickled the sides of her mouth. "We seem to sign a lot of peace treaties over these little suckers."

"That's because neither of us can stay mad at the other. I like you, Shannon, even if you are a pain in the butt."

"Same to ya, Kane."

He sat down on the end of the bed and tugged her

down beside him, glad they were on friendly terms again—at least for the moment.

Leaving distance between them, Shannon curled one bare foot beneath her, revealing hot-pink toenails. Funny how appealing five naked toes could be.

"There's something I've been wanting to talk to you about."

"Besides sex?" She batted her eyes at him while crinkling the candy wrapper in one hand.

"My second favorite subject—horses."

Taking the sucker from her mouth, she studied it. "You can't work with Domino."

"Fine. That wasn't it anyway." He wanted to tell her that a little conditioned-response would work wonders on Domino, but she didn't want his advice—yet.

She ran her tongue over the lollipop. Jackson forced his gaze away, determined to keep his mind on horses. Now, while they were at peace, was as good a time as any to broach the subject of his workshops.

He took a deep breath and jumped in. "I want to conduct a training symposium this fall."

A line appeared between her eyes. "What does that mean?"

"Bring in clients who want to learn to handle their horses better. Teach them the reasons horses behave the way they do. I'll give lectures in the round pen using the clients' animals to show the proper training techniques." Warming to the topic, he stood up, moved to the window and looked down to where his dream was waiting.

"We could even record the workshops and sell the video tapes."

He turned, hoping his enthusiasm was enough to convince Shannon that his idea was worthy. But instead of acceptance, her eyes flashed anger.

"What are you trying to do?" She pointed the sucker at him. "Make me and my grandfather look like fools for the way we've been training horses for years?"

Shocked, he hadn't considered that Shannon would consider the clinic an insult to her ability as a trainer. "It's not like that, Shan."

He reached out, tried to touch her. She yanked away.

"I won't have it." She shot off the bed. "And neither will Granddad."

"I've cleared it with him already."

"Behind my back?" He could see the fury working its way inside her. So much for a truce.

"He owns the ranch. It was his decision to make."

"And just who will take care of the ranch while you're playing the big-shot horse whisperer? The stable hands certainly can't take on the load. That's why we hired you. We need you training those horses, making money for this ranch, not spending all your time on your own agenda."

"My workshops will help the ranch, Shannon. Don't you get it? The more interest we generate for my training clinics, the more horses we'll be asked to board and train."

"Somehow you've scammed my poor old sick grandfather into agreeing, but don't expect me to help."

Now she'd made him mad. He was a lot of things, but he didn't cheat.

"Let's get one thing clear, Shannon. Gus is one of the wiliest businessmen in this county. And since our wedding he's started taking charge again. No one is going to hoodwink him into anything." He didn't add that Gus did a little conniving of his own.

Some of the steam hissed out of her. "All right. I shouldn't have said that. But, darn it, Jackson, it's embarrassing to have people clamor for you to work their horses when this is my ranch."

Oh man, there was that insecurity again. What was she going to do when she discovered he now owned an interest in her training facility?

"You're a good trainer, Shan. An excellent horsewoman. If only you'd let me teach you—"

But Shannon wouldn't hear another word. Robe flapping, she wheeled and stormed toward the bathroom. "I can't stop you from doing this, Kane, but don't expect my help."

Right before she slammed the door, she threw the Dum-Dum at him.

Shannon had a headache. Two of them to be precise. Her Cajun husband and a spotted gelding. Neither wanted to do things her way.

Approaching the recalcitrant horse, she prepared for the usual battle as Domino tossed his head and shied backward. He hated taking the bridle. Eventually, if she applied enough of the right kind of pressure, Domino would submit to her will. Jackson, on the other hand, never would. Maybe that's what made him so enormously attractive. He refused to be tamed.

And every time they were alone for more than thirty seconds, he kissed her. Trouble was, she wanted him to. She liked his kiss, his touch. Not only that, but she was starting to like a lot of other things about him, too.

For all his devil-may-care facade, Jackson worried about his aunt and her granddad. He made frequent trips to see Bonnie and they talked on the phone almost every day. And he did everything possible to make running the ranch easier on Gus while letting the old man remain in charge.

Shannon also admired the way he treated the other ranch hands, as well as the rapport he had with clients. Most of all, she liked the nights they lay in bed and talked.

He'd told her of his family or rather lack thereof, of his days on the rodeo circuit with Jett Garret, of his desire to be among the best trainers in the country and of the work he'd done to get there. In the intimate darkness, he'd shared his goals in such passionate terms that Shannon knew he would succeed. Jackson Kane was not the shallow boy he had been at twenty, a disconcerting notion to say the least.

Jackson's future was on the rise, reason enough for her to protect her heart, so that when the time came to let him go, she wouldn't be shattered.

She felt badly about the fight they'd had over the up-coming clinics. She'd overreacted, feeling personally af-fronted by the suggestion that she wasn't as good a trainer as he, but the truth was right in front of her—Jackson knew things she didn't. He had a magical rap-port with horses that she hadn't mastered in a lifetime of horsemanship. And regardless of her protestations, plans for the training event had gone forward with Gus's total support.

Flyers, mailings, Internet ads and word of mouth had generated considerable interest already. Jackson's reputation with difficult mounts was spreading. Too stubborn to admit she might—just might—be wrong, Shannon felt left out of all the preparations.

"You and I are two of a kind," she said to Domino. "Hard heads who expect our own way and end up worse off because of it."

The horse's ears flicked. Shannon studied his glossy brown eyes and read the intelligence there. Domino was trying to understand what she wanted but couldn't quite get it. Somehow he had gotten his signals confused and didn't know the appropriate response.

Ruefully, she shook her head. "Now I sound like Jackson. Next thing you know I'll be bending my hand in a claw and pretending to be a predator."

She had a quick mental flash of Jackson gentling a head-shy colt. In a matter of days, the colt was coming to Jackson, eager to accept the halter and the human hand against his face.

"What the heck? Might as well give it a try. No one but you and me will ever know."

Recalling Jackson's notion that horses respond to the relief of pressure rather than its application, she draped the lead rope over her left arm and approached from the side, her left hand raised. As expected, the horse tossed his head, but after an interminable amount of time while Shannon waited, hand in the air, Domino relaxed his neck. Immediately Shannon lowered her hand. Then she repeated the procedure again, forcing herself to be patient.

Normally, she would have tied his head, forced on the bridle and been about her business. This horse-whispering stuff was work.

Intent on her effort, constantly alert to the smallest alteration in Domino's body language, Shannon heard nothing but the sound of the paint's soft breathing. When Jackson's voice came from behind, she nearly jumped out of her skin.

"Trying to steal my tricks?" As she swiveled her head in his direction, Jackson tilted the brim of his hat. "Not bad for the first time."

Shannon stepped away from Domino and lowered her hand. "I didn't hear you come in."

Amusement set his dimples dancing. "Figured as much."

"I was just—don't be thinking—" she sputtered, looking for a way to deny the obvious.

"Aw, come clean, Mrs. K." He slouched against a stall

and crossed his arms. "You've finally come to your senses."

"Maybe about one or two things." A lot of things in fact, but she wasn't ready to throw in the towel completely.

His amusement changed to pleasure.

He removed a lollipop from his mouth and studied the shiny red ball with intentional carelessness. "Care to help me in the round pen today?"

She'd been thinking about it. He was going to do this clinic thing with or without her. She might as well go along for the ride and pretend it had been her idea from the git-go. "Maybe."

"I could use your help." He stepped closer, black eyes serious. "Come on. What do ya say? I need you, Shan."

She knew he was talking about more than horse training, but the idea that Jackson would admit needing anybody, especially her, shot a thrill through her veins.

"Really? You need me?" Wouldn't hurt to make him beg a little. She'd swallowed her pride. Let him swallow a little.

He extended his hand, palm up. "Yeah."

Shannon placed her hand atop his and felt his strong fingers close around hers. The sense of rightness was startling. She and Jackson, hand in hand, a team.

And that's how easily Jackson lured her into helping with the Kane's Horse-sense Clinics.

Chapter Seven

On a fall Saturday when the wind was calm and the sky was blue enough to taste, horse trailers rumbled onto the Circle W Ranch for the first-ever Kane Clinic.

With excitement buzzing in his blood, Jackson moved quietly among the horsemen and women, shaking hands, chatting. Some men would be nervous, but he wasn't. He'd spent his entire adulthood working toward this day. He'd trained with the best, and even though he had been born with a natural affinity for horses, he'd spent countless hours perfecting his methods and learning more about the language and character of his four-legged friends.

His future was upon him and he was ready.

Horses whinnied, a sound he relished. Trailer doors clattered and truck engines roared. Across the grass, his beautiful wife led a dapple-gray toward the round pen where he would be conducting the first session. He turned in her direction and felt his gut clench in response. Just looking at her stirred up a whirl of disturbing emotions.

Guilt, first and foremost, because Shannon didn't know that their frustrating charade of a marriage was responsible for his dream coming true. Admiration for the way she'd jumped in and worked her pretty tail off to help him, though she'd pretended to resist all the way. Exasperation, because after three months they were still sleeping in the same bed like strangers.

But under all those feelings lurked something even more worrisome. He was getting attached to his stubborn bride. Not love, mind you, but affection, sort of the kind he felt for his horse. Sort of. He liked waking up beside her and talking to her just as much as he enjoyed kissing and teasing and trying to get her into the sack. Considering his duplicity, as well as his opinion of marriage, that was a dangerous road to travel.

He hated to think of how she would react should she discover what he and Gus had done. She'd be furious, but she'd be hurt, too. Better to make her believe that he had gradually purchased an interest in the ranch than for her to ever know that Gus had given it as a dowry for marrying her.

As much as he disliked the lie between them, Shannon would be more hurt by the truth than by his silence, and so his deal with Gus would have to remain a secret forever.

"Hey, Cajun boy." Blond hair shining in the sunlight, she smiled at his approach. The horse strained toward him in greeting, blowing softly through his nostrils for attention. "Looks like a great turnout."

Her fancy jeans had flowers down the sides, but it was the brown suede shirt that drew his attention. She'd left the top three buttons undone, and the flash of creamy skin made him salivate.

To keep his hands off Shannon, he put them on the gray horse, stroking the soft neck in slow, circular motions. "I'm pretty pumped." That was an understatement.

"You don't show it."

But he could if she'd let him.

"Don't want to spook the horses." He winked, then nudged his chin toward the round pen. "About time to get started. Any final words of advice?"

"No need. You know your stuff. You'll be awesome."

At her praise, a fierce swell of absolute confidence surged through his chest. It was good to have someone believe in him other than himself.

He knew he shouldn't, considering the direction of his earlier thoughts, but the imp on his shoulder forced him to say, "A kiss for luck then?"

"Got it, Cajun boy." On tiptoe, she pressed her mouth to his and sent a sizzle down to his boot heels.

If he'd been salivating before, now he was reduced to panting like a dog. He backed off and patted rapidly at his chest. "No fair giving the teacher a heart attack."

As if his kiss didn't affect her in the least, she glanced around the barnyard, a small pucker between her eyebrows. "Speaking of hearts, have you seen Granddad? I don't want him overdoing."

"He'll be fine, Shannon." In fact, Jackson suspected that Gus had never been quite as debilitated by his illness as he'd let on. Since maneuvering Shannon into a marriage that pleased him, the crafty old rancher had made a remarkable recovery. "I saw him with Bonnie up at the house."

She glanced in that direction. The movement parted the opening in her shirt. "Is your aunt chasing after my grandfather?"

"Looks that way."

"Good."

They both grinned, and then Jackson bent for another quick kiss. "Talk to you after the first session."

But before he let her walk away, he buttoned two of her shirt buttons.

Shannon watched him go, a little hitch beneath her ribs. The taste of his cherry candy lingered on her lips and her Cajun cowboy lingered in her mind. The skin of her chest tingled from that slight, momentary brush of Jackson's hand as he'd buttoned her shirt. She didn't know why he'd done that. Nothing showed. But sometimes men were so hard to understand. Especially this one.

Who would have thought the day would come when she'd stand on the sidelines and cheer while Jackson Kane taught horse lovers his horse-whispering ways? And who would have thought she'd be so proud and excited for him?

After a minute, she took the horse inside the facility and then found a place among the spectators.

Out on the dirt-floor pen, Jackson began his first workshop. Shannon gripped the top of a fence rail, stomach jumping with anxiety. Maybe Jackson was calm and collected, but she wasn't. She wanted so badly for him to succeed.

He looked magnificent, all six feet four inches of him, standing next to the handsome buckskin. She'd helped him select the bright red, long-sleeved shirt that set off his dark skin to perfection, but nature had provided him with a body that looked incredible in snug jeans, black leather chaps and snakeskin boots.

Using his favorite horse, Hombre, he demonstrated his philosophy of training horses with love, understanding and positive conditioning. Shannon had heard his spiel, seen his notes and watched him go through the routines time after time in preparation for this day. She'd even helped him prepare, but seeing him in action thrilled her to pieces.

"There are certain universal truths in training a horse properly," he said. "The first is safety for both you and your animal. If you hadn't noticed, a horse is a lot bigger than you."

A chuckle of amusement rippled through the group of onlookers as Jackson continued. With gentle humor and quiet confidence, he talked of conditioned response, of training with kindness instead of force, of getting inside the horse's head, all concepts Shannon would have mocked a few months ago.

But by the second session it was clear that Jackson's students not only agreed with him but thought he was a miracle worker. One after another, he took unfamiliar horses into the ring and won their confidence, amazing both their owners and the rest of the crowd.

The redhead standing beside Shannon was no exception. "I wonder if he gives private lessons," she said. "Did you see anything in the brochure about that?"

"Private lessons?" Shannon shook her head. "I don't think so." Not if he wanted to live to do another clinic.

"I think I'll ask him after this session." The woman laughed. "He's not only a great teacher, he is one hot cowboy. I wouldn't mind being alone in a barn with him."

Shannon couldn't hold the words back any longer. "That hot cowboy is my husband."

"Oh." The redhead looked disappointed. "Well. Congratulations. You're a lucky woman."

"Yeah, I guess I am," she said slowly, marveling at the sense of pride she experienced in the admission.

Jackson's good looks and easy manner would win him more than one female fan. And she had a bad feeling that beautiful cowgirls would be an increasing temp-

The Silhouette Reader Service™ — Here's how it works:

Accepting your 2 free books and gift places you under no obligation to buy anything. You may keep the books and gift and return the shipping statement marked "cancel." If you do not cancel, about a month later we'll send you 4 additional books and bill you just $3.57 each in the U.S., or $4.05 each in Canada, plus 25¢ shipping & handling per book and applicable taxes if any.* That's the complete price and — compared to cover prices of $4.25 each in the U.S. and $4.99 each in Canada — it's quite a bargain! You may cancel at any time, but if you choose to continue, every month we'll send you 4 more books, which you may either purchase at the discount price or return to us and cancel your subscription.

*Terms and prices subject to change without notice. Sales tax applicable in N.Y. Canadian residents will be charged applicable provincial taxes and GST. Credit or debit balances in a customer's account(s) may be offset by any other outstanding balance owed by or to the customer.

If offer card is missing write to: Silhouette Reader Service, 3010 Walden Ave., P.O. Box 1867, Buffalo NY 14240-1867

NO POSTAGE
NECESSARY
IF MAILED
IN THE
UNITED STATES

BUSINESS REPLY MAIL
FIRST-CLASS MAIL   PERMIT NO. 717-003   BUFFALO, NY

POSTAGE WILL BE PAID BY ADDRESSEE

SILHOUETTE READER SERVICE
3010 WALDEN AVE
PO BOX 1867
BUFFALO NY 14240-9952

GET FREE BOOKS and a FREE GIFT WHEN YOU PLAY THE...

SLOT MACHINE GAME!

Just scratch off the silver box with a coin. Then check below to see the gifts you get!

YES! I have scratched off the silver box. Please send me the 2 free Silhouette Romance® books and gift for which I qualify. I understand I am under no obligation to purchase any books, as explained on the back of this card.

310 SDL D72Q

210 SDL EEWJ

FIRST NAME

LAST NAME

ADDRESS

APT.#

CITY

STATE/PROV.

ZIP/POSTAL CODE

Worth TWO FREE BOOKS plus a BONUS Mystery Gift!

Worth TWO FREE BOOKS!

Worth ONE FREE BOOK!

TRY AGAIN!

www.eHarlequin.com

(S-R-02/06)

DETACH AND MAIL CARD TODAY!

tation to a man as virile as Jackson. But he was her husband. Hers.

The sudden slap of jealousy shocked her.

Moving away from the redhead, she went to stand next to the arena floor, closer to Jackson. As she watched her husband do his thing, the truth appeared before her like an opening flower—truth she'd denied for ten years, three broken engagements and a summer of growing up the hard way.

She was in love with Jackson Kane.

She'd never been able to marry anyone else because a certain footloose Cajun cowboy had always owned her heart.

The strength of that love filled her with a wondrous female power. She wanted to write it in the sky, shout it to the world. She loved him. He was her husband. She was his wife. And, by glory, it was time to do something about it.

At the end of a long but satisfying day, after the clients had driven away, after Gus and Bonnie had disappeared to who knew where, after sharing a meal Bonnie had left in the oven, Shannon stood beneath the shower's hot spray contemplating today's momentous decision.

Jackson, tired and dirty, but too hyped up for sleep, had showered and gone into the office to make some notes. Tempted to follow, she'd waited, giving herself time to prepare...or to back out.

Though her mental alarm system screamed code red,

Shannon shut the warning off along with the shower knob. She was a big girl now, not a frightened eighteen-year-old who didn't know what she wanted out of life. She knew what she wanted, all right. She wanted Jackson, her make-believe husband.

Jealousy had opened her eyes to the truth. And though she had no idea what the future held for the two of them, she knew one thing. As long as Jackson remained her husband, she was going to make the most of it. She'd loved him for ten years and she'd love him a hundred more. Having him now was better than never having him at all.

Going to the dresser, she took out her sexiest nightie, but quickly shoved it back inside. "Too obvious."

She'd bought the silky confection during one of her engagements thinking a negligee would help her get past the fear of commitment. It hadn't. She'd never worn the thing.

After another moment of indecision, she took the garment out again and slipped it over her head, surprised to see her fingers tremble over the satin tie.

At the mirror, she spritzed cologne, dabbed her lips with peachy gloss and brushed her hair over her shoulders. Her heart thudded painfully and her throat felt as dry as a Texas summer. If she didn't calm down, she'd ruin everything.

She threw the brush down in self-disgust. "This is ridiculous."

Struggling against uncharacteristic shyness, she considered waiting for a better time, waiting for him to make the first move. Then she heard Jackson's tread on the stairs and knew the wait was over.

Summoning all her courage, she took a deep breath.

"Now or never, cowgirl," she muttered and turned just as the door opened.

Jackson froze in the doorway, dark eyes widening. "What's this?"

Her heart hammered but she didn't even consider backing down. She struck a pose. "Like it?"

His nostrils flared. He swallowed hard, sending his Adam's apple into a curtsy. "Where's your long gown? You can't sleep in that."

The wary, near panic-stricken statement gave her the courage she needed to move toward him.

"I don't plan to. Sleep, that is."

Wariness turned to bewilderment. "Am I missing something?"

She tiptoed her fingers up his chest and draped both hands over his wide shoulders. Then she let her voice drop to a sexy purr. "I hope not."

As understanding dawned, a slow, knowing grin broke over his face and set his wonderful dimples into relief. He skimmed his hands along her sides, leaving an entire family of goose bumps behind. Shannon shivered with delight.

"Mind telling me what brought this on?" Jackson nuzzled the top of her head. "Not that I'm complaining, mind you."

Shannon met his gaze and answered as honestly as she dared. "I'm tired of fighting the frustration."

He blew out an enormously happy sigh.

"Well," he said. "It's about danged time."

And then his mouth found hers, and they were lost.

Later, as she lay with her head upon his chest, listening to the steady drum of his heart, Shannon was a whirlpool of emotions. Joy, pleasure, contentment and love so profound she wanted to shower him with kisses and say the words over and over again.

But she knew better. As painful as it was to keep such a beautiful thing hidden, Shannon knew Jackson's views on love and marriage. They'd made a pact, a commitment not to get permanently involved. He'd run like a scalded cat at the slightest inkling that she could no longer keep her end of the bargain. Love was the one thing that would drive him away.

Too happy to follow that line of depressive thinking, Shannon concentrated on the here and now. For this day, this moment, all was well.

Circling a finger over the hollow in his throat, she murmured, "You were a big hit, Cajun boy."

His voice took on a sexy, teasing tone. "You were pretty awesome yourself."

She bopped him on the shoulder. "I'm not talking about *that*."

"Ouch." Chest rumbling with laughter, he replied, "There goes my fragile ego."

"There is nothing fragile about your ego."

He shifted beneath her, drawing her down beside him so they lay face-to-face.

"It was a good day, wasn't it? Everyone seemed impressed."

"Especially the women."

He feigned innocence. "I didn't notice."

"Yeah, right. Like you didn't see that redhead with the cazonkas out to there. She stuck them right in your face."

Again that rumble of laughter. "Jealous?"

"No."

"Liar."

"What makes you so sure?"

He stroked her hair, expression serious. "You're in this bed, in my arms, where I've been trying to get you for three months. I figure there has to be a reason why you chose tonight."

She shied away, suddenly uncomfortable that Jackson could see inside her so well. If he guessed the truth… "The time seemed…right. A celebration of your success, I suppose."

Studying her face for a long moment, Jackson drew in a deep breath, then released it slow and easy. The wholly contented sound filled Shannon with a sense of rightness.

"Whatever the reason," he said, "you came up with the perfect ending to a perfect day."

Shannon propped up on one elbow and grinned down at him. "Who said it was over?"

He reached for her, his grin slow and wicked. "Not I, said the big bad wolf."

With a squeal of laughter, Shannon flung herself across his chest.

Chapter Eight

The weeks following the clinic were a wonderful, anxiety-ridden time for Shannon. Every time Jackson looked at her or touched her, she let herself believe their marriage was real. Even knowing the danger of that game, she was amazed at her capacity for self-delusion. Jackson may not ever be a real husband, but loving him had brought out a domestic side she hadn't known existed.

Jackson's aunt Bonnie, her narrow face flushed, handed a bowl of steaming vegetables to Shannon. "I sure hope you don't mind me takin' over your kitchen this way."

"Mind? I'm grateful." Shannon slid the creamed peas onto a table already laden with homemade biscuits, roasted potatoes and a succulent pot roast. "Do you know how many years Granddad and I have tried to cook for each other? And now poor Jackson has to eat our cooking, too? Having a real cook in here is a treat. I'm sure your nephew will agree."

From the adjacent living room came Gus's laughter and the rumble of Jackson's voice. Shannon ached with love for the two most important men in her life.

"Well," Bonnie said, oblivious to Shannon's thoughts. "I've been promising to make Gus my special chocolate turtle cake for a month, and he finally insisted I get on with it before one of us died." With a cheery laugh, the spry little woman bustled around the kitchen like a twenty-year-old. "Isn't that just like him to say something so silly?"

Shannon turned from setting out the plates, affection for her grandfather's lady friend strong. "You've been good for him, Bonnie."

"I was so worried you'd be upset about us seeing each other, me being so much older than him and all."

Shannon stifled a laugh. At seventy-four Bonnie had more energy than Gus had ever had. "You've put a spring back in his step."

"Oh, go on with you." Bending over the stove, Bonnie slid a dark cake from the oven. The rich scent of chocolate filled the air. "I think we're ready. Tell those two to wash up."

After they'd gathered around the table and Gus had offered grace, dinner conversation flowed.

"Bonnie," Gus said. "This is the finest meal I've had since the last time I ate at your house."

Bonnie flushed a becoming pink. "That was yesterday, you goose."

Grinning, Gus winked at Jackson. "I like it when she blushes. Cute as a button, ain't she?"

Jackson and Shannon exchanged knowing glances. Sparks were definitely flying between the older couple. Shannon had to admit she was glad. Gus was happier and seemed to feel better ever since that first dinner Bonnie had prepared for all of them shortly after Jackson had returned to Rattlesnake.

Who would have thought that a jar of sweet pickles and a single meal would lead to this? She, Shannon the commitment shy, head over heels in love with a man she would have run over with a truck a few months ago. Now, just looking at his darkly handsome face and snapping black eyes made her insides go wild.

Dimples dancing mischievously, Jackson leaned over to murmur in her ear. Beneath the table, his hand found her knee and massaged seductively.

"All this romance in the air gives a man ideas."

Sure enough, her insides reacted. Little jolts of pleasure tingled all the way to her belly button. "I don't think you need any help in the idea department," she whispered back.

While pretending to concentrate on a particularly succulent slice of roast beef, Shannon slipped off her shoe and rubbed her foot up and down Jackson's calf. Two could play at this game.

With a chuckle that drew the older couple's attention, Jackson withdrew his hand and reached for one of Aunt Bonnie's golden biscuits. He looked so innocent Shannon grabbed a swig of tea to keep from laughing.

"How's the blood pressure, Gus?" Jackson asked, buttering the roll as though he and Shannon weren't tormenting each other under the table. Just for orneriness, Shannon rubbed his thigh. He slanted a warning glance in her direction that said she would pay. Shannon couldn't wait.

Before Gus could swallow his pot roast and answer Jackson's question, Bonnie spoke up. "Dr. Torrence says for Gus to keep doing whatever he's doing." The two elders exchanged twinkling glances. "Because it works. She's never seen anyone recover so quickly."

Shannon's stomach took a nosedive. She removed her hand from Jackson's leg.

The marriage charade had succeeded beyond their wildest dreams. Granddad was convinced that she and Jackson were a perfect match, and his health was on the upswing. Shannon was grateful for that blessing. More than grateful. But any mention of her grandfather's health served as a sharp reminder of why she and Jackson had married in the first place. They'd married, not so she could live a fantasy and play house with this handsome Cajun, but so her grandfather would get well.

But her marriage of convenience was a temporary deal. How long would Jackson be willing to continue the charade now that Granddad was on the mend? What would happen to her grandfather's health when Jackson was tired of playing?

And what would happen to her?

The longer they were together, the more she loved him. Maybe she shouldn't wait for Jackson to grow tired of her. Maybe she should end it herself while she could still survive in one piece.

Whistling a nameless tune, Jackson unloaded another feed sack from the back of his truck, dumped it inside the feed room and went back for another. An October breeze stirred the dust and he paused to study the sky, hoping for rain.

A stable hand mucking out a stall leaned his pitchfork against the wall and trotted over. "I'll unload the rest, Jackson. Miss Shannon is looking for you."

Jackson glanced around expecting to see Shannon's shining blond head pop out of a stall. "Where is she?"

"Up at the house. She wanted you to look over that stock contract with her."

He didn't know what had come over Shannon since the day of the clinic, but after a month of terrific nights and great days, he sure enough appreciated the change. Oh, she was still a pain in the butt, sassy and argumentative, but she was different, too. Man, was she different.

Stripping off his leather gloves, he slid them into his back pocket and started toward the house. Four months ago, Shannon was trying to run him off, and now she was asking his advice.

But then he was different, too. He wasn't straining at the bit of marriage the way he'd expected. All things considered, he was actually pretty content. That was good. The longer he could deal with the confinement of being married and tied down to one spot, the better for everyone. Aunt Bonnie's house payments were almost caught up. The training workshop had been such a success he was already planning several more in the spring. And the increase in requests for his and Shannon's training expertise kept them both hopping.

Yep. For now everything was good. He would know when the marriage was over, when Shannon was tired of him, and when he was ready to take his training clinics on the road. Sometimes he wondered where this ill-considered game would lead, but right now he would hang on for the ride. When it was over, he would cut his losses as he always had and move on down the road.

Shannon opened the back door and waved at him. The action pulled her tank top up above her belly button, sending his stomach southbound. He quickened his pace.

Yep, one of these days he would have to end it. But not today.

Cool October turned to frosty November. The snows would soon blow through the Texas Panhandle, but as Shannon stared at the small blue stick in her hand, a cold wind was already blowing in her mind.

Ever since the night of Jackson's symposium, she'd been halfway expecting this to happen and halfway hoping it would. Anyone who played with fire was bound to get burned. And they had played—a lot. All her thoughts of ending the marriage had remained just that—thoughts, worries, fears. And she'd played on, pretending that her husband loved her as much as she loved him.

Torn between elation and terror, she picked up the phone to call Dr. Torrence. She wouldn't say anything to anyone, not even her best friend, Becka, until she was sure.

But if she was pregnant, this changed everything. Would Jackson stay this time? Or would a baby be the proverbial straw that broke the back of her make-believe marriage and sent her husband running?

She touched her belly protectively, heart thundering like a herd of wild horses. A baby. After all this time of aching for the one she'd never known, Shannon wanted this child so much.

But she wasn't fool enough to believe that Jackson would feel the same.

Two days later, wiping his boots at the back door, Jackson tossed his hat on an end table and went in search of Shannon. She'd disappeared earlier in the day without a word, but he'd seen her SUV pull into the drive a few minutes ago.

Gus was nowhere around, a fact that brought a smile. Aunt Bonnie must have strong-armed him into working on the leaky faucet at her house. Jackson had offered to fix it, but she'd smiled and said Gus could handle the problem.

Seeing his widowed aunt happy and cared for meant everything. She had loved him when his own mother hadn't, and had put her life on hold to raise him. If he was any kind of man at all, he owed it to Bonnie.

Unwrapping a Dum-Dum, he paused to toss the paper in the garbage and heard a soft mumble coming from the ranch office. Shannon. He'd found her. And his entire body reacted at the thought of seeing her, touching her, listening to her sass him about something. Who would have thought Jackson Kane could get so worked up over the same ornery woman day in and day out?

Pushing the door open, he saw her standing behind the desk, one hand on the telephone. She must have been on the phone just now when he'd heard her voice.

She glanced up, spotting him, and his gut clenched at the serious-as-death expression on her face. Except for the day Gus had gone down with his heart, Jackson had never seen Shannon so serious. She was ornery, she was sexy, she was a royal pain the butt, but she wasn't one to get upset over nothing.

"What's up?" He wasn't sure he wanted to know.

She swallowed, bluebonnet eyes filled with anxiety. "Sit down."

Like a black widow spider, a really bad feeling crept up his backbone. "Why?"

"Because I just got a call from the doctor's office."

"Gus?" He gripped the edge of the desk. "Is he—"

"I'm pregnant."

He didn't sit down. He collapsed. Everything inside him jumped around like frog legs in hot grease. "Should I get the gun?"

She gave him a quizzical half smile. "What?"

"Aren't you going to shoot me?"

"Don't tempt me."

"I think I already did."

"Yeah, well I did my share."

"No kidding." She'd tempted him plenty, but he wasn't one to put up much resistance.

He dragged a hand over his face. A baby. Shannon was pregnant with his baby. He stole a glance at her flat-as-the-Texas-landscape belly. "The deal is off. You know that, don't you? We're staying married."

"People don't always stay married just because there's a baby."

"They do where I come from." By now he'd regained his composure, stalked across to where she stood and tried to take her into his arms. He knew about abandonment, knew how it was to grow up without a parent. There was no way that would happen to his kid. "Any woman who gets pregnant by me will be taken care of by me."

She backed away, her face pale. "Really? Then where were you the last time?"

He froze, bewildered. Surely, she didn't mean what he thought she meant. No way.

"What are you talking about?"

She pressed her lips together and shook her head. Tears the size of hen eggs pooled in her gorgeous blue eyes. "Never mind. I didn't mean to say that."

"Oh, no you don't. You can't drop a bomb like that and then back off."

She sucked in a deep breath and slashed at the tears now flowing down her cheeks. Her stubborn chin raised a notch. "When you drove off with Jett Garret ten years ago, I was carrying your baby."

All the air went out of him. "Oh, God."

"Yeah well, I did a lot of praying, let me tell you." She emitted a small laugh that held not a drop of humor. "But I was eighteen and my prayers were for all the wrong things."

Jackson felt as though he'd been kicked in the gut by an angry stallion. "Why didn't you tell me?"

"By the time I'd thought it through and realized you had a right to know, it was too late."

"Too late? I don't understand. How could it ever be too late? Unless—" A horrible, unbearable thought entered in his head. "You didn't—" He couldn't make himself ask if she had terminated the pregnancy, but the horror must have shown on his face.

"Have an abortion? Why? Would you have cared?"

"You know I would have, so get that idea out of your head right now." A hideous realization struck him like a fist. "You are not aborting *this* baby. A father has rights. You're my wife, for crying out loud!"

"We don't have a real marriage, Jackson. We had a deal. And I won't go back on my word."

"This is a baby, Shannon. That's a lot more important than a deal." He'd beg if he had to. "If you don't want him, let me have him. But don't do this."

She clenched her fist, posture rigid, blue eyes glacial. "You don't know me at all, do you, you arrogant, pig-headed Cajun?"

He flopped back into the chair and stared up at the ceiling. "I don't know anything right now except you're pregnant and planning to have an abortion. And I can't let you do it."

"Why?"

"Because…" Because he was scared to death of the feelings he had for her, because he wanted to be a daddy, though the idea made his knees quake, because he hated the thought that she'd done it once before. But he couldn't say any of that. Shannon didn't give a flip about him or his feelings. She wanted him gone. And she wanted their baby gone, too.

"Because we can make it work. We may not love each other, but we can raise this baby together and be a family. He deserves that from us."

She was trembling and tears flooded her cheeks. Whether she wanted him or not, he had to hold her. She kept putting the desk between them, but he edged around the massive structure and took her into his arms.

Now he knew why she'd been distant and preoccupied the past couple of weeks. She'd suspected the pregnancy and blamed him.

"I'm sorry, Shan. Don't be mad. Don't do anything crazy."

She struggled against him, but when he refused to release her, she went limp in his arms.

"I didn't get rid of our baby, Jackson. I lost him." Her voice broke on an agonized whisper. "I lost him."

Relief, followed by a stunning sense of loss, ran through him as racking sobs broke from her throat. She hadn't terminated the pregnancy. She'd miscarried.

"It's okay, sweetheart. It's okay." Sorrow filled him for the lost child he would never know and for the young girl who'd faced a tragedy alone. He should have been here.

Scooping her into his arms, he carried her to a chair where he sat and held her on his lap like a hurting child. He hadn't been here then, but he was here now and not about to let her suffer again. He pressed her close, letting her sob out the pain she'd bottled up for ten years. His shirtfront dampened from her tears.

When she was empty, he dried her face and let her sit up, but he wasn't ready to release her.

"Want to tell me about it?"

She dabbed a Kleenex against one eye. "Not much to tell. I was probably about six weeks and had just begun to suspect the truth. Becka and I bought one of those home tests. I was so scared. I cried and cried. And I prayed a lot trying to figure out exactly what to do, how to tell Granddad, what to do about you. Three days later it was all over."

"Does Gus know?"

She shook her head, worrying the tissue between her fingers. "Only Becka. She took me to Dr. Torrence as soon as the cramping started, but by the time we got there the baby was gone."

"That's not going to happen this time," he said with a vehemence that startled them both. "You're going to see an OB doctor right away. And you're going to take it easy, take care of yourself."

Her smile, though tremulous, made him feel better. "Are you going to try to boss me around just because I'm pregnant?"

Ah, good. She was getting sassy again. She'd be okay.

"You're danged straight I am." As gently as he knew how, Jackson laid a hand on her stomach. "We made a baby, Shan. We have a responsibility."

"I know." Sniffling, she emitted a sound somewhere between a sob and a laugh. "Who would have believed that you, of all people, would be discussing responsibility?"

"Kind of scary, ain't it?" Real scary if he thought about it too much. He rubbed her red nose with his. "What do you think? Do I look like a daddy to you?"

Shannon's puffy, reddened eyes pretended to study him. "Not even close."

He hooked an elbow around her neck and drew her against his stampeding heart.

A baby. His insides shook just thinking about it. He was going to be a daddy.

Man, did that ever complicate things.

Chapter Nine

A cold Panhandle wind swirled around her feet as Shannon worked with a high-spirited bay filly. Seldom cold, despite the threat of snow, Shannon unbuttoned her work coat and welcomed the cool air against her shirt. She loved the outdoors, loved the wind blowing through her hair and the feel of a horse in her control.

At three months along, the baby still remained more like a dream than a living being. And yet, seldom a minute went by that Shannon didn't think about the tiny life growing within her and feel a leap within her spirit.

"Guess what, Star," she murmured in a soothing voice as the filly danced away from her. "I'm having a baby."

A thrill raced through her blood, more warming than any jacket. Since the day she'd told Jackson, her love for the handsome Cajun had grown by leaps and bounds.

Instead of the rejection she had expected, Jackson had gone overboard to see that she and the baby were well cared for. At times, he could even be too doting for her independent nature, but his attention was too sweet to resist. Gus, of course, was overjoyed to know he would be a great granddad.

The familiar niggle of worry poked at her. Where would this all end? Gus truly believed she was happily married to a man who loved her and would always care for her. In fact, at the announcement of the pregnancy, Gus had startled her by announcing his intent to sign over an interest in the training facility to Jackson as a gift. And what could either she or Jackson say? They couldn't admit that the marriage was a farce.

And what of Jackson? Because of the pregnancy and now the training facility, he was trapped in a marriage he'd never wanted. Love wasn't something that could be forced by circumstances. And Shannon was no fool. Jackson didn't love her. He liked sleeping with her, but that was far different than this incredible joy she felt for him.

Shannon's mind wandered, thinking, worrying. The filly, a magnificent, high-spirited beauty, took advantage of the inattention and backed away from the halter rope, shaking her head up and down. Star was destined to be a fabulous show horse if Shannon could work out the nerves and teach her to handle properly. Brought back to attention, Shannon approached the animal to bring her under control.

An annoyed voice ripped through her concentration. "What do you think you're doing?"

At the unexpected sound, Shannon yelped and whirled. Startled, the filly reared, pulling Shannon off her feet. Still clinging to the lead rope, Shannon slammed belly first into the dirt. The horse, frightened now, whinnied wildly and tried to buck.

In two seconds flat, Jackson's shadow fell across Shannon as he positioned himself between her and the flailing hooves of the out-of-control animal. Shannon, pulse thundering against her temples, fear for her baby uppermost, instinctively rolled to one side to escape danger. She sat up, panting and shaken, and leaned her forehead against her knees.

With his back turned, Jackson couldn't see that she was out of harm's way. Wide shoulders intentionally relaxed and in control, he advanced toward the panicked horse, trying to regain the lead rope.

"Let her go, Jackson." Shannon forced her voice to a calm undertone. "I'm out of the way."

"Hush and stay back," he answered in that same soothing whisper he always used with the animals.

If she hadn't been so frightened, she would have been angry. Fact of the matter, she *was* angry. How dare he tell her to hush? He was the one who'd caused the problem.

In a matter of minutes, Jackson calmed the horse enough to approach her. Star's flesh quivered and gleamed with sweat, but she allowed the cowboy's touch. Her eyes, the whites showing, watched every move he made.

After a bit of stroking and murmuring, Star relaxed…and so did both trainers. Dusting her jacket, Shannon started to rise when Jackson pivoted and pointed a finger at her. "Don't move."

His face was a thunderstorm. Okay, he was upset. So was she. Pulling her knees back to her chest, the cold, hard ground numbing her behind, she waited while he took the horse inside the barn. If he wanted a fight, she was ready—as soon as she stopped shaking.

"What do you think you're doing?" he said again as he exited the barn.

She hitched her chin higher, refusing to be intimidated. "You asked that already."

Standing over her, hands on his hips, scowling like a bulldog, he looked enormous. "And I didn't get an answer."

"I was doing what I have done all my life—training a horse."

"Not anymore you aren't. Not the ones with a dangerous temperament."

"Excuse me?" Shannon was gripped with a sudden fury, fueled more by the near miss with Star than anything Jackson had done. "I don't remember asking your permission."

He jabbed a finger at her. She slapped it away.

"Don't point your finger at me, cowboy," she said, knowing her reaction was childish but too shaken to care.

The finger returned, this time within inches of her nose. "That's my baby you're carrying."

Shannon covered her belly protectively. No need for him to know how frightened she'd been that something *would* happen. "This baby is perfectly healthy and so am I. A simple fall will not hurt either of us."

"How can you be so sure? After the last time, I'd think you would be more cautious."

Shannon gasped, fingers pressed to her lips. Was he blaming her for the miscarriage? "I would never do anything that would harm my baby." Extending a hand that, to her annoyance, trembled the slightest bit, she said, "Stop acting like an idiot and help me up."

Instead of complying, Jackson came down on his haunches in front of her. Faded blue jeans stretched taut over long powerful thighs. His voice softened. "Didn't the doctor say the first few months were crucial? That you were more likely to miscarry then than later?" His big hand covered her stomach. "Are you sure the baby's all right?"

She nodded, not wanting to look at him. Not wanting him to know how much she needed him to care about her as well as their child.

"I'm past the first trimester now, Jackson. You can stop fretting like an old mother hen."

"Your face is dirty."

His strong fingers brushed her cheek, but Shannon leaned away from his touch. She couldn't think straight or stay angry when he touched her. "Don't ever sneak up on me again when I'm working."

"I don't want you to work—at least not around the horses." The corner of his mouth lifted. "They're bigger than you."

The old joke didn't fly. "Don't smother me, Jackson. You go your way. I go mine. That's the deal."

She didn't know why she felt compelled to push him.

"Neither of us is going anywhere." He stood up, pivoting away from her. "That deal has been off since the day you got pregnant."

"It doesn't have to be." Why, oh why had she said that?

"No? Is that what you want?" He glanced over one shoulder, expression empty. "For me to leave?"

Shannon's insides trembled. How had the conversation gotten to this point?

"Is that what *you* want?"

He stared off into the pasture without answering for such a long time that Shannon's hope shattered. He wanted to leave but was duty bound.

When he turned around, he offered a hand and helped her to her feet. His thoughtful gaze went to her belly.

"I can't even tell you're pregnant."

What did that mean? Did he think she had lied about the pregnancy to trap him? "I can get proof if you want it."

He blinked at her, expression puzzled. "What?"

"Never mind." With a shake of her head, she turned away, anxious to escape a conversation that had somehow gotten so far out of hand. Something was happening to her reason. She wasn't thinking straight today.

Jackson caught her upper arm and stopped her. "I

don't doubt you're pregnant, Shannon. Is that what you thought? That I didn't believe you?"

"It crossed my mind." And, heaven help her, the idea hurt so bad she wanted to cry.

Jackson's dark eyes studied her. "Why? You never wanted this marriage any more than I did. Why would I think you'd lie about being pregnant?"

She shrugged away from him, trying to weasel away from the truth as well. If she wasn't very careful, she'd blurt out her feelings. She wanted this marriage so much, and if he knew she loved him he might suspect the pregnancy was an intentional device to trap him. "I don't know. Hormones, I guess."

"I guess." He tilted her chin, forced her to look up at him. His voice softened. "I was thinking about how small you are, Shan, not questioning the pregnancy. Shouldn't you be getting pudgy by now? How can the baby be big enough to be healthy?"

When he was gentle like this, all Shannon's resistance flew away with the north wind. She wished with everything in her that Jackson would take her into his arms and hold her. She didn't want to fight. She wanted to love and be loved.

"My OB doctor says everything is progressing normally. The baby is fine. He's small right now, but strong and healthy." And so am I, she wanted to say. But Jackson wouldn't care about that.

"But wouldn't he do better if you rested more instead of putting him in danger around these animals?"

"If you hadn't come storming out here, the mare wouldn't have freaked."

Jackson blew out a breath and looked heavenward. "Okay, I overreacted, and I'm sorry for that. Real sorry. But seeing you handle a horse we both know is flighty scared me. Still does."

"Dr. Dean says I can continue doing everything I've always done."

Jackson frowned. The wind caught the sides of his sheepskin coat and buoyed them out from his body. Shannon longed to step inside and wrap her arms around his middle. "Maybe you should see a different doctor."

She laughed, though not from joy, and wrapped those lonely arms around her own middle instead. "Jackson, have you ever watched a mare run when she's pregnant?"

"Sure."

"And her owners ride her, too, don't they?"

He didn't look too happy with her logic. "I guess so."

"Get the point?"

"You're not a mare."

"Thanks for noticing," she said with much more sarcasm than she felt. "But the theory is the same. Females of all species are built for carrying their young. The doctor says the miscarriage was just one of those things that happens sometimes, and there is no reason to believe it will ever happen again. I want this child with all my heart and would never do anything that jeopardizes his well-being. Never."

"Will you be more careful then?"

"Absolutely." The filly had done more than scare her. She'd made Shannon realize how easily she and her baby could be injured. "If it will make you feel better, I promise not to work around any of the skittish or un-broken horses—if you will promise to stop hovering."

Dark eyes studied her long and hard before he reluctantly replied, "All right."

"Deal?" She offered to shake on it.

He stared at her palm and frowned. "You skinned your hand."

Exasperated, she asked, "Is it a deal or not?"

"Sure. Whatever." Frowning, he draped an arm around her shoulders and pulled her to his side. "Better get you in the house. Wouldn't want junior to catch cold." He stopped and looked down at her. "Is that possible? Can an unborn baby get sick?"

"I don't know."

"We're taking no chances. In the house and out of this wind right now."

Shannon bit back a groan as she snuggled against his side, their fight thankfully relegated to the past. Jackson's fussing over the pregnancy drove her nuts, but she was glad he cared about their baby.

If only he cared as much for her, too.

"He's still driving me nuts, Becka."

Shannon had kept her word to be more careful, but Jackson hadn't kept his.

Sitting in Becka Garret's living room, Shannon

sipped at a steaming mug of hot chocolate and let herself whine. At five and a half months pregnant she felt cranky and hormonal. Who better to dump on than her best friend in the whole world?

She mocked Jackson's commands in a singsong voice. "Put your feet up. Go lie down. Take care of my baby."

"I think it's kind of sweet that Jackson is so enamored of you and this baby."

"He's not enamored of me, Becka. I could almost enjoy the attention if that were the case. He's only doing this for the baby." Regardless of how nonchalant she tried to sound, the words trembled on her lips. "Not me."

"Shannon Gayle." Becka's cocoa cup clinked in the saucer. Her eyes widened in sudden understanding. "Why didn't I see this before? You're in love with him."

"Isn't that a laugh? Me, in love with a man I'd sworn to hate forever." Though she'd protected the secret as carefully as she'd protected her baby, Shannon was relieved to finally share the news with someone. She'd known that eventually Becka would guess. Too bad Jackson wasn't as astute.

"You know what I think?" Becka squinted as though she could read Shannon's mind. "I think you've always been in love with that big ol' handsome Cajun. That's why you could never find the right guy."

"And I think you know me too well." Carefully, placing her own cup on the coffee table, Shannon said, "You know Jackson, too. And the one thing he never wanted was to be married. Oh, sure, he'll take responsibility for the baby, but the marriage was make-believe, a short-term agreement to get Granddad back on his feet and off my case about finding a husband."

Becka leaned back on the plaid couch, a tiny pucker appearing between her brown eyes. "I thought this temporary marriage thing was called off."

"It was, sort of. But that's the very point. Jackson wants to stay together for the baby, not because we love each other." She waved her hand ineffectually. "Sometimes I'm jealous of my own child. Isn't that sick? Because Jackson loves him and not me."

"Are you sure about this, Shannon? From what you've told me, Jackson seems very attentive. Men don't behave that way without a reason."

"Because of the baby, Becka. Not me." The depressive thought settled on her like dust in a Texas sandstorm.

Becka nibbled the corner of a cookie and then aimed it in Shannon's direction. "So. How's your love life? Yours and Jackson's, I mean. Still hot as ever?"

"Becka!"

The redhead laughed. "Well, if Jackson is still interested in the bedroom, he can't be thinking entirely about the baby."

"Maybe. But then he's a male. They're all interested in sex." Sure, he was attentive, affectionate even, and there were times she almost believed he cared. Then he'd go and say something about their pretend marriage and spoil the illusion.

To change the subject, she stuffed the last bite of a

snicker doodle into her mouth and said, "These cookies are good." She reached for another. "Did you make them?"

Becka shook her head. "No. Cookie did. Even though he is officially Colt's cook and not ours, he can't resist taking care of us."

"You're lucky to have him."

"Yeah." Becka smiled. "Cookie is a born nurturer, but he doesn't want anyone to know that he's a softy. He was so upset when Jett and I built this place and moved out of the main house. He thought we would starve to death." Her laugh was full of affection. "So he trucks up here at least once a day to bring goodies and make certain we are feeding Dylan properly."

The Garret cook and housekeeper was a gruff old navy man with a heart of gold and a laugh that shook the rafters.

"Speaking of Dylan. Where is he?"

"He went with his daddy to look at a new bull."

Shannon was happy for the glow of love shining on her friend's face. "Who would ever have thought that Jett Garret, the wildest man in Rattlesnake, would settle down and be a daddy?"

"Not me. At least not at first. But Jett loves Dylan as if he was his first dad instead of his second."

"And he loves you, too," Shannon said, glad that her friend had found a second chance at love after the tragic death of her first husband.

"Oh yeah. He loves me." Becka's expression went all soft and dreamy. "And I love him more than I ever thought I'd love anyone. Two years of marriage and I still get a leap in my heart when I hear his voice. Jett will always be unpredictable and a little crazy, but there is no doubt that Dylan and I come first. Remember that, Shannon. If Jett can fall in love and become such a fabulous, if somewhat unorthodox husband, so can Jackson."

Shannon sipped the sweet chocolate, thinking about the unhappy, uptight woman Becka had been before freewheeling Jett had come along. God knew what he was doing when he put the two of them together.

"Any more escapades lately?" Becka never knew when Jett would come in the door and whisk her off to some sort of breathtaking adventure. Parasailing, sky-diving, deep-sea diving. They'd done them all and more.

"Nothing since the trip to Mexico at Christmas. With Dylan in school now, we're waiting until summer so he can go along. Unless…"

A clatter of voices and the sound of footsteps interrupted their conversation. "That must be my boys now," she said.

Sure enough, a handsome cowboy with a small boy riding piggyback loped into the living room. The child's giggle filled the house with joy.

"Where's my woman?" Jett Garret exuded enough energy to fuel a nuclear submarine.

"Where's my mama?" Dylan echoed.

With a laugh, Becka rose to greet them, taking Dylan into her arms to receive a quick, childlike smack on the lips. Then he slithered off Jett's back, snitched a couple of cookies and disappeared down the hall.

Jett lingered, kissing his wife long enough to make her blush and to make Shannon wish that Jackson looked at her with that same besotted expression.

"Hi, Shannon." Arm looped casually around his wife, he turned his attention to the guest. "You're looking…pregnant."

They all laughed. Smoothing down her oversize sweatshirt, Shannon pooched her belly out. "Is that what this is?"

Becka, ever the nurse on duty, frowned at the small protrusion. "How much weight have you gained?"

"Five pounds." The volleyball around her middle felt much larger.

"Not much. What does your OB say?"

"Now you sound like Jackson." Shannon patted her tummy. "Dr. Dean says I'm all baby, and he or she is healthy and thriving."

Jett perched on the couch arm, munching a snicker doodle. "Got my old traveling partner worrying about you, huh? Who'd have ever thought it?" He winked at Becka. "Two old rodeo bums mad about their women."

Jackson had never confided the truth to his rodeo buddy, and Shannon certainly wouldn't.

Becka, bless her, saw Shannon's discomfort and jumped in to help. "Jett honey, would you get Shannon and me some more cocoa?"

His mock scowl was fierce. "Do I look like the domestic type to you?"

"More and more every day." She batted her eyelashes playfully.

With an exaggerated sigh, Jett took the mugs. "I knew this would happen if I married her. Why couldn't I have taken her up on that hot affair she offered?"

With a laugh and the quick reflexes of an athlete, he dodged the couch pillow flying his way and headed for the kitchen. The pillow hit the piano leg with a soft *whump*.

"Gracious, I love that man. Our lives would be perfect if—" Becka caught herself and stopped, but not before Shannon saw the flash of sadness in her friend's eyes. They'd had this conversation more than once in the last year. Now she suffered a twinge of guilt because she had what Becka wanted so badly.

"You'll get pregnant one of these days, Becka. Give it some time."

"Two years. Isn't that time enough? We've never done anything to prevent me from getting pregnant and yet I'm not. We wanted Dylan to have siblings while he was small enough to be close to them. At this rate, he'll graduate college first."

"Just…keep trying." The platitude was feeble at best.

Jett's head appeared around the doorway. "That's what I tell her. If at first you don't succeed…" He wiggled his eyebrows at his wife. "Ready when you are, darlin'."

He disappeared again, but Shannon appreciated his intention. He teased and joked about the situation because he didn't want Becka to be unhappy.

"You married a good guy."

"The best. And so did you."

"Does it bother you that I'm pregnant when you can't be?"

"How can you ask me that after all we've been through together? You were the one who propped me up when Dylan's father was killed. You coached me through Dylan's birth, and I was there when you miscarried. We've weathered the bad times and the good ones. Don't you dare shut me out of this wonderful time in your life. I'm not that fragile."

"Okay. Consider me well chastised. Besides, who else would I whine to but you?"

"I don't consider your concerns whining. This baby you're carrying is everything you ever wanted." Becka held up a hand. "Don't deny it. You may not have realized the truth until now, but this is what you've been waiting for all your life. Jackson and this baby."

"If only…" Shannon let the thought slide. What good would it do to wish for something so completely outside her power. "I can't stay married indefinitely to a man who doesn't love me."

"Can't or won't?"

"Both. I need to be loved, Becka. You understand that, don't you?"

"Of course I do." Leaning forward, Becka placed a hand atop her friend's. "I'll return your advice, Shannon. Don't give up. Keep trying. Maybe he loves you already and doesn't know it yet. Maybe he needs time to come to grips with all that's happened. Have you considered telling him how you feel?"

Horrified, Shannon recoiled. "And let him step all over my heart again? No thanks. I'd like to at least keep my pride intact."

"Pride isn't a very cozy playmate. But if you can find what Jett and I have, it will be worth all the effort."

"Don't worry. I don't give up easily. My baby deserves parents who love each other." Shannon rose, gathering her purse along with her courage. "Sometimes when Jackson is rubbing my back or massaging my feet—"

"He does that!"

Shannon put a finger to her lips and glanced toward the kitchen. "Don't tell Jett. Jackson would be mortified."

"Girlfriend, there is more going on inside Jackson Kane than love for that baby. No man massages a woman's feet without having feelings for her."

"You think?" Oh, she hoped Becka was right.

"It's certainly a good sign." Becka offered a quick hug. "Now go home, be your sexy, amazing self and tell that man how you feel."

On the thirty-minute drive from the Garret Ranch to the Circle W, Shannon thought about Becka's advice. Perhaps her friend was right. Perhaps she should tell Jackson that she was in love with him and see what happened.

As she pulled into the driveway, the porch light came on. The tall Cajun stepped out onto the porch wallowing a sucker stick in his mouth. A sharp March wind snatched at his shirtsleeves. Leaning against the porch post, he removed the sucker and pointed it at her.

Shannon went all mushy inside. The big ape. She was nuts about him. Why couldn't he love her back?

Exiting the car, she marched up on the porch, grabbed the sucker out of his hand and kissed him full on the lips. He tasted like strawberry and cold wind.

After a surprised laugh, Jackson groaned and folded around her like a blanket, returning the kiss with a passion that curled her toes. She lost her grip on the sucker and it pinged against the porch floor.

Waltzing her backward, Jackson pinned her against the wall and rained kisses down her neck. She shivered with pleasure. With Jackson's wide body to warm her, the Texas winter didn't exist.

When they finally came up for air, Shannon murmured, "Where's Granddad?"

"Where else? Bonnie's." His voice was deep and throaty.

"How very convenient." She slanted her eyes upward, toward their room. "Shall we?"

Jackson pulled back and frowned down at the bulge around her middle. "I don't know, Shan. Maybe we shouldn't anymore."

The chill wind rushed in to replace his warmth. "Why not?"

"The baby." He shifted uncomfortably. "You know. You're pretty far along now. I wouldn't want to hurt him."

Sliding her arms over his shoulders, Shannon nuzzled his neck. If she was going to tell him, the timing must be perfect. "Dr. Dean says it's okay."

"You sure?" To his credit, he looked ridiculously hopeful.

"Absolutely." She cranked her eyebrows up and down. "I asked."

A slow grin eased up his cheeks, sending his dimples into overdrive. "Then what are we waiting for?"

He scooped her into his arms as if she weren't carrying a few extra pounds, kneed the door open and trotted up the stairs.

A long time later, feeling as content as a cream-fed cat, Jackson trailed his fingers lazily over Shannon's silky shoulder. She lay curled against him, her hard little belly fitted into the curve of his side.

"Did you have fun at Becka's today?" he murmured.

"Yeah." Her soft breath puffed sweetly against his neck. "I've missed seeing her lately."

"If going out there puts you in this kind of mood, I want you to go every day."

She chuckled softly. "Can't. Too far and too much work to do around here."

That again. She'd slowed down, cut back on the physical labor, but if he had his way she'd do nothing at all until after the baby was born. "Gus and I did all right without you."

They could have used her help with one of the foaling mares, but he didn't tell her that. She was magic in those situations.

"Cookie made snicker doodles."

He grinned down at her. The semidarkness painted her pretty face in shades of shadow and cream. "Bring me any?"

"Sorry. I brought me instead."

"Can't complain about that." He moved one hand to her belly and made gentle circles on the mound that held his son or daughter. Lately, he'd become fascinated by Shannon's body, not that he hadn't been before, but this was different. The changes amazed him, made his stomach lift as if he'd taken a hill too fast. Sometimes his chest ached from thinking about the baby inside her.

He didn't tell Shannon that either. She'd probably laugh, a macho cowboy talking sappy that way.

Voice lazy and muted, Shannon stroked his jaw with one finger. "Jett was there."

"How is the old sidewinder?"

"Happy as a hog in a mud wallow."

They both chuckled at Gus's favorite saying.

Without warning, the belly beneath his hand gyrated. "Whoa. Did you feel that?"

She laughed. "A kickboxer has taken residence inside my belly. Of course, I feel him thrashing around in there. He's very active tonight."

"Is that good?"

"Very good. He always wakes up about the time I want to go to sleep."

He smiled on the inside. "Preparing you, isn't he?"

"And you, too. You're taking your turn getting up in the night."

"I can handle that. Occasionally." Not that he minded, but Shannon didn't need to know how easily she could take advantage of this budding paternal instinct of his. He was having a hard enough time with it himself. "Shouldn't we be buying him a bed soon? And something besides that handful of tiny little clothes you keep folding over and over again?"

"No rush. I thought we might take a trip into Amarillo later this spring and do some shopping."

"I hate shopping."

Playfully, she bit his chin. "You're going."

He knew he would. "Should we wait that long? With the baby coming in July—"

"Plenty of time. I want to paint the nursery first."

He'd experienced a mix of thrill and terror the day they'd moved the junk out of the extra bedroom and declared it the nursery. Somehow the action confirmed that he was really going to be a daddy, something he'd never planned to be. He'd planned his future, his career, but not this. Fate had dealt a different hand.

"I'll drive into Rattlesnake for some paint tomorrow."

"No hurry. Let's wait until after the ultrasound when we know what we're having. That way we can choose the color accordingly."

"Do we have to find out? I like the idea of a surprise."

She raised up on one elbow to peer at him in the semidarkness. "Really? Me, too."

"Cool. Then let's ask them not to tell us. We'll find out together on the day he arrives."

"Maybe he will be a she."

He laced the fingers of his free hand through Shannon's hair. Her scalp was warm and the silky mane was a pleasant contrast to the work-roughened texture of his skin. He could go on touching her forever.

"A she is good." Actually, a baby girl with Shannon's blue eyes and stubborn chin would be excellent, but a boy would suit him, too.

The thought gave him pause. What was happening to him lately? He wanted to make a name for himself, to train horses, to be successful, not raise kids. Even though he had clinics planned for this spring and his expertise was becoming more in demand, he'd never wanted to be stuck here permanently.

After the baby arrived, he'd have to make some decisions. But tonight, with Shannon's soft skin brushing his and a spring storm brewing outside, he'd focus on the here and now.

"What color should we paint the room?" Shannon murmured, oblivious to his tumultuous thoughts. "Yellow?"

"Sissy color."

She tickled his chest hair with her fingertips. "How about purple or green or red?"

"Don't we have to do a baby color?"

"He's our baby. We can have anything we choose."

He liked that idea. "What's your favorite?"

"Red. And yours is blue." How had she known that? "So let's do red, white and blue with stars and ponies floating around the room."

"Perfect."

"I'm glad we settled that." With a contented sigh, Shannon snuggled against him once more and was quiet.

They lay in comfortable silence for a while, the room dark except for the light from the bathroom. Jackson had almost drifted off to sleep when Shannon whispered, "Hey, Cajun boy."

"Mmm, hmm?"

"I want to tell you something."

"Shoot."

She was silent for a long time while Jackson tried to decide if she was stalling or had fallen asleep.

"Shan?" he whispered, fighting the pull of la-la land until she'd said her piece.

"You made me very happy tonight."

"I did?" What was that all about? Paint? Or sex?

"Yeah." She stirred a tiny bit and he heard her swallow. "Good night, Jackson."

"Night." At last, he could drift off. He closed his eyes.

"I love you."

His eyelids sprang open. He was wide awake now, adrenaline spurting through him so fast he could catch a thoroughbred in full lope.

Love? She was in love with him? That wasn't supposed to happen. They were pals, buddies, partners.

Well, okay, lovers, too, and pretty darned hot ones at that. But *in* love? No way.

He stared up at the ceiling wishing an alien spacecraft would fly over and beam him up.

Shannon couldn't love him. They had a deal. Even if he had called the deal off for the sake of the baby, he still had a deal with Gus. Shannon could never know about that. Ever. And love required a certain honesty he couldn't give any more than he could give his heart.

Oh, man. Now what was he supposed to do?

Coward that he was, he feigned sleep.

Chapter Ten

"Morning, sunshine," Gus greeted as Shannon entered the kitchen. Outside, snow fell and the wind howled, but inside the house was cozy and the coffeemaker sent out a wonderful aroma.

"Morning, Granddad." She breathed deeply, savoring the scent because she couldn't have the drink. "The one thing I miss most is my morning coffee."

Her granddad was seated at the table, yesterday's newspaper spread before him. She bent to kiss his smooth-shaven cheek. Eyes on his paper, he patted the side of her head.

"I'm about ready for a refill." He handed her his cup. "Where's that man of yours?"

"He'll be down soon." And what would she do then? How would she face him after last night? After the way he'd rejected—by his silence—her declaration of love.

Opening a cabinet, she took out the Bisquick. "Want some pancakes?"

"Sounds good. Fry up some of those little sausages, too, will you, hon?"

"Okay." She took the links from the refrigerator and tossed them into a skillet to brown while she stirred up the pancake batter. "But you're really not supposed to eat all that fat."

"I'm going to anyway so quit nagging. Doc says I'm doing so good she might take me off my blood-pressure tablets."

"What about your heart?"

"The old ticker is still working." He patted his chest. "Maybe not as good as it used to work, but that's what the little white pills are for."

"Any spells lately?" With all the time he spent away from the ranch at Bonnie's house, Shannon was no longer able to keep a close eye on him. But she didn't worry anymore. Bonnie did a better job than she had ever been able to do.

"Not a bad spell in ages," he said, the paper rattling as he turned the page. "Last one was on Christmas, remember?"

How could she forget? "You got too wound up when Bonnie slipped on the ice."

"Scared me. I've taken a shine to that old woman."

"Really? I would never have guessed," Shannon

said mildly. Spatula in hand, she turned from the stove to look at her grandfather. She'd swear he almost blushed.

Gus grinned sheepishly at her and shrugged. "You think I'm a silly old man, don't you?"

"I think love at any age is a beautiful thing. You'd better grab her before some other smart man does."

"Been thinking about it. Wanted to talk it over with you first."

"There's nothing to talk about, Granddad. You do what makes you happy and I'll be happy. That's the way it's supposed to be when you love somebody."

She slid a stack of golden pancakes onto a plate, added a couple of the forbidden sausages and set breakfast in front of him.

He patted her arm. "I reckon I raised you right after all."

Heart full, Shannon hugged his shoulders just as Jackson sauntered into the kitchen.

"Something smells good." He headed to the coffeepot and poured a steaming cup.

"Pancakes and sausages," Gus answered around a mouthful. "Want some?"

"Sure. But I'll fix them. Shannon shouldn't be on her feet." The carafe clinked onto the warmer. Back still turned, he stirred sugar into the cup.

"Fiddlesticks. She's healthy as a horse."

Turning, Jackson leaned his backside against the counter, expression serious. Shannon's heart stuttered, then tumbled to her toes.

She whirled back to the stove. "I'll make your breakfast."

"You don't have to." Tension, thick as the clouds outside, hung between them. If one of them didn't break the ice soon, Granddad would notice.

Gus's paper rattled. "I told you, son. Let her cook. It makes her happy."

Out of the corner of her eye, Shannon watched Jackson shove away from the cabinet and move in her direction. "Anything to make the lady happy."

She grabbed for the pancake batter and poured. A hiss of steam rose from the black skillet just as Jackson leaned over her shoulder. The front of his body grazed her backside.

"Mornin'," he murmured, so close to her ear goose bumps prickled her flesh.

Shannon thought her heart would pop out of her chest and into the fry pan, even though she knew what he was doing. Playing the part for Granddad's sake.

"Good morning." Her greeting sounded as stiff as the icicles hanging outside the window. She flipped a pancake and wished he would go away. Facing him was difficult enough without him hovering.

"Sit down. Your breakfast will be ready in a minute."

"Terrific." His tone was light, breezy and so indifferent she wanted to cry.

Ambling to the table, he scraped back a chair and sat, accepted a section of the paper from Gus, and asked, "You think this snow will let up later?"

If she hadn't been so hurt and humiliated, Shannon would have picked a rip-roaring fight. The arrogant Cajun acted as if nothing unusual had occurred last night. As if she hadn't opened her soul to him in a way she'd never done for any man. She considered using the spatula as a slingshot and hurling pancakes at him.

Instead, she shoved the pain away and slapped the hotcakes onto a plate. Fine. So he didn't love her. No surprise there. Baby or not, she had known that from the start. Just because she'd been fool enough to fall in love with him didn't mean he was obligated to return the favor.

If he could ignore something as important as love, she could pretend the words had never been said. Somehow, she'd get over him.

And after the baby came, she would release Jackson from his obligations and let him go. Yes. That's exactly what she'd do—even if it killed her. Life was too short to live with a man who didn't love her.

By late May, Jackson's conscience was killing him. Out of the blue. Just like that. He'd awakened this morning, looked into Shannon's sleepy blue eyes, and down at the seven-and-a-half-month bulge around her middle, and developed a nagging conscience.

Since the night she'd whispered her love in the darkness and he'd pretended to be asleep, trouble had been brewing inside him. He had ignored the problem as long as possible, but now here it was, full blown. His conscience screamed for him to do something about the subterfuge between him and Shannon. He never should have agreed to a share of the training facility under any circumstances, but certainly not as some kind of secret dowry deal.

Jamming a box knife into cardboard, he ripped open the carton that held a wooden crib. Yesterday he and Shannon had taken the trip to Amarillo, bought the crib and a lot of other stuff. Afterward they'd gone to dinner and a movie where Shannon had laughed so hard at Jim Carrey, Jackson had thought she'd go into labor. Once he'd put a hand on her belly and the other over her mouth. His actions had only made her laugh harder—after she'd bitten his palm.

Grinning at the memory, he slid the side rails away from the cardboard and propped them against the wall.

They'd had a terrific time yesterday. So much fun that Jackson couldn't imagine being with any other woman—ever. But he'd seen the way she looked at him now, the hurt she tried to hide and the love she couldn't. Neither had mentioned that night again, but the memory hung between them, ever present. She loved him and the idea scared him cross-eyed. Why, oh why had she messed things up this way?

Guilt was like a toothache, throbbing at him all the time. Shannon would die of humiliation to know how he'd played the role of a double agent. Sure, back then, he'd thought he was doing a good thing for everyone concerned—help Shannon, help Gus, help himself. Now he saw how screwy the entire idea had been from the outset. Everybody lost on this deal—no one more than Shannon.

Digging in the cardboard box, he came up with a package of screws and springs and bolts. If he hurried, he could have the crib up before she returned from the grocery store. She liked surprises. Hadn't she squealed like a kid over that saddle he'd bought her for Christmas?

On his haunches, he found the instruction sheet and tossed it to one side. Why did companies waste paper on instructions? Any man with half a brain could put together a baby bed.

The springs on the side rails gave him the most trouble, but after a few choice words, a scraped knuckle and thirty minutes, he stood back to admire his handiwork. Not bad for the first time he'd ever touched a piece of baby furniture.

His gut clenched. *Man*. A baby bed. His baby's bed. He flopped onto the floor and pulled a hand down his face. How had things gotten so screwy?

In a couple of months, a real live miniature person would occupy this room and his life forever. Something had to be done about the lies that had created this marriage and ultimately this baby. No kid of his would grow up believing he was an afterthought. He'd been there and had the empty hole in his heart to prove how much a parent's mistake could hurt a child.

Looking around the nursery at the crisp white walls, the blue-and-red border with matching curtains and the shiny new baby furniture, Jackson made a decision. He'd have a talk with Gus, call off their deal. Though it would take years, he'd pay for his share of the facility instead of having it handed to him for marrying the owner's granddaughter. He couldn't give Shannon those three little words, but he could do this for her—and for their baby.

Quickly cramming leftover trash and a couple of extra screws into the now empty carton, he went in search of Gus.

He didn't have to look far. The old cowboy was in the ranch office, poring over the books.

"Checking to see if I'm cheatin' you?" Jackson joked as he entered the room.

Gus looked up, eyes twinkling. "Nope. Just appreciating how much money you've made me this year."

"Couldn't have done it without your ranch."

"Yours, too, now."

"That's what I wanted to talk to you about. Sort of."

Gus closed the ledger and leaned back in his padded chair, studying Jackson with a speculative look.

"Sit down then. And tell me what's on your mind."

Jackson took a straight-backed chair, whirled it around and straddled it. Fiddling in his pocket, he pulled out a Dum-Dum, lemon flavored.

"Want one?" he offered.

"Nope. Bonnie's fixin' Creole chicken."

"Can I go with you?"

Gus laughed. "You didn't come in here with that

mulish look on your face to talk about Bonnie's cooking."

"No. I didn't." Searching for the right words, he sucked in a breath. The scents of leather and Shannon's vanilla candle swirled into his nostrils.

"This about my granddaughter?"

He exhaled. "Yeah."

"You two fussin'?"

How did he get his point across without exposing the other lie in this mixed-up marriage? The lie he and Shannon had told Gus.

"It's not that. It's just—I want to call off our deal. Give back my share of the ranch until I've earned it. Let me make payments on it, whatever. I can't go on with this lie hanging between Shannon and me."

"Shannon would be suspicious for sure if you did that. She'd start asking questions. And if she found out about our bargain she'd be brokenhearted, not to mention mad as a she-bear." Gus rubbed the bridge of his nose. "Look, son, her getting pregnant was a sign that we did the right thing."

Gus had a peculiar way of seeing things.

"I'm not so sure. But I *will* admit you were pretty clever, making her believe you gave me that interest in the ranch because of the baby."

"See what I mean? She never needs to know that I signed that paper the day before you married her." Gus rolled his chair back from the desk and rose. "A deal is a deal, son. I've kept my end of the bargain. Now you keep yours. Stay married to my granddaughter, raise that young'un and train all the horses you want. That's the only way I see to keep Shannon from ever finding out that I bribed you into marrying her."

Shannon stood in the hallway outside the office, hand over her mouth to keep from crying out. Her face burned and blood rushed against her temples with such force she thought she was having a stroke. Over and over again, the conversation between Jackson and Granddad played in her head. They'd betrayed her. Both of them. The two men she loved more than anything had lied to her, had conspired against her. All this time she thought her marriage was for Granddad's sake. Instead, Jackson had used her for his own gain.

Her entire body trembled and her heart hammered relentlessly. A vile-tasting sickness rose in her throat as she backed toward the stairs.

Rushing silently up to her bathroom, she splashed cold water on her face and breathed slowly in and out, trying to regain her composure. The baby inside her, so big now, reacted to her emotional turmoil. She stroked her middle with both hands, hoping to calm both mother and child.

"Oh, baby. What are we going to do?"

Her first reaction was to leave and never come back. Maybe she would leave, at least until she had some time to think things through. She needed to talk to someone she trusted.

"Becka," she whispered to the white face in the mirror.

Inside the closet was a small overnight bag already packed and waiting for the trip to the hospital. Taking the bag, she scribbled a note telling Jackson she wasn't quite the fool he thought her to be. She tossed the paper onto the bed where she and Jackson had made love, choked down a sob and hurried out of the house before he discovered her presence.

Disappointed that his conversation with Gus had not brought the hoped-for results, Jackson trudged upstairs to fetch his hat and gloves. Might as well get some work done while he stewed. Sooner or later, he'd find a way out of this ridiculous bargain with the devil. Not that Gus was the devil, but any time a man went around making career deals that affected his wife and baby, he was asking for trouble.

In seconds he was running down the stairs, Shannon's note in hand. "Gus!"

Gus must have heard the panic in Jackson's voice because he met him in the living room. "What is it? The baby? Shannon?"

"She knows." He handed Gus the note, choking on the next words. "She's gone."

"Gone? Where?"

"I don't know. She only says she's leaving, that she can't live with me anymore under these circumstances." He should have understood her feelings but he didn't. All he could think of was the unbelievable pain searing him like a hot poker. Shannon was gone. She'd left him.

"Go get her." Gus slid down onto the sofa, his face ashen. "Bring her home."

"Didn't you read the note? She doesn't want me." Just like his mother, Shannon had abandoned ship when the going got tough. He'd tried to make things right for her sake and yet, she'd left him. "This marriage was a mistake from the start."

"Nothing that can't be fixed. Give yourself a chance at love, boy. It's worth the trouble."

"Love?" He shook his head in denial. Poor Gus. Poor blind fool who thought love was the answer to everything. Jackson Kane knew better than to fall for a woman who would up and leave him. Especially one who could drive away with his unborn baby.

"I don't think so, Gus. She doesn't want me. Not from the very beginning." And the realization stabbed like a sharpened pitchfork.

Turning on his heel, Jackson trudged upstairs and collapsed on the bed, boots and all. Shannon would scold him for that—but Shannon was gone.

Heaving a shuddering sigh, he tossed an arm over his eyes and tried to think rationally.

He wanted his child. Heck, he even wanted Shannon, though that made no sense at all considering what she'd done. He could stay and fight it out. But staying meant risking his heart, something his mother should have cured him of long ago.

Or he could protect himself from hurt and walk away from the scariest, most incredible thing that had ever happened to him.

For once in his life, he had a decision to make that was far bigger than his career dreams ever could be.

Chapter Eleven

"Tell me what's happened. You're shaking like a leaf."
Becka pushed Shannon onto the sofa, shoved a glass of
tea into one hand and a Kleenex into the other. "Did you
and Jackson have a fight?"

Too shaky to drink anything, Shannon set the unwanted tea on the coffee table. She strangled the
Kleenex in her palm, refusing to let the hot tears fall.

"Much worse than a fight. The truth."

"The truth? About what?" Becka frowned. "Honey,
you're not making sense."

"You already know why Jackson and I married."
Shaking her head, Shannon gave a mirthless laugh. "Or
why I thought we married."

"Because of Gus?"

"Yeah. Well, surprise, surprise. He and Jackson were

in on some kind of conspiracy the whole time. The marriage had nothing to do with Granddad's health as I thought. The real truth is—" The vile words were hard to say, even to her best friend. "Granddad *hired* Jackson to marry me."

"He what!"

"You heard me." Shannon's insides twisted with the awful knowledge. "Granddad was so convinced I needed a husband that he offered Jackson a part interest in the training facility in exchange for marrying me. And Jackson agreed."

Considering her own bargain with Jackson, she shouldn't have felt so betrayed—but she did.

"Did Jackson actually confess this to you?"

"I overheard the two of them talking. They were gloating about how they had fooled me. When Granddad found out I was pregnant he made a big deal about signing over part of the ranch to Jackson as a gift because of the baby."

"Nothing wrong with that."

"Becka, the papers were signed the day before our wedding, not after I became pregnant."

"You heard them admit this?"

"Yeah. The gift was a sham." Humiliated beyond words, Shannon picked at the Kleenex as an excuse not to make eye contact. Even with her best friend, she suffered shame at the admission. "A sham, just like my marriage."

"Wait a minute. Let's back up and think this through. You know what they say about eavesdroppers."

"And it's true. They never hear anything good."

"Maybe you misunderstood. You're upset right now, in shock. Maybe there's more to this than you're seeing."

With the compassion that made her an excellent nurse, Becka moved to Shannon's side and slid an arm around her waist. Becka, no bigger than a sixth grader, stretched her arm as far as it would go and still couldn't reach around Shannon's pregnant belly. The ridiculous sight broke through Shannon's melancholy and she giggled.

"Look at us. An elephant and a peanut."

Becka returned the grin. "You are not an elephant. A duck maybe if the waddle is any indication…."

Shannon, feeling a tad bit better, sniffed. "Gee, thanks, friend. I knew I could depend on you."

"And you were right." Giving Shannon's nonexistent waist a quick squeeze, Becka turned sideways on the couch. "That being the case, I'm about to give you some unsolicited advice."

Guessing the direction of Becka's thoughts, Shannon held up a stop-sign hand. "I'm not going home. Not yet, anyway. First, I have to come to grips with the fact that Jackson does not and never will love me for me. He cares about the baby. He cares about the horse ranch. But he is not in love with me."

"Have you asked him?"

Shannon hedged. "Not exactly."

"Okay, then. That's your answer. *Talk* to the man."

Becka had no idea that Shannon had confessed her love to Jackson only to have him pretend the words were never spoken. That kind of rejection was hard to share with anyone. Asking Jackson to express his feelings was out of the question.

Jett Garret chose that moment to saunter into the living room. "She's right, you know. Usually is."

He bent to kiss his wife.

"Jett," Becka spluttered. "You are not supposed to be listening to this conversation."

"Too late." His grin was at least a hundred watts and completely unrepentant. "Already did." He slouched into the chair across from the women and aimed his question at Shannon. "What do you know about Jackson's family?"

Unsure what the rest of the Kane family had to do with this conversation, Shannon lifted her hands, then let them drop. "Only that it's very small. Just his great-aunt Bonnie and him since his dad died a few years ago."

"Wrong. Somewhere out there Jackson has a mother."

Surprised, Shannon blinked. "He never mentioned her." One more secret he'd kept from her.

"He wouldn't. The subject of mommy dearest is way too touchy." Jett propped a booted foot on one knee. "You didn't hear this from me. Jackson has a lot of pride, you know. But back in the old days when Jacks and I used to get a little rowdy on occasion, he would sometimes get maudlin. Cry in his beer, so to speak."

Shannon exchanged looks with Becka. "He's not usually the whining type." In fact, she'd never heard him complain about much of anything.

"True. But tequila is amazing stuff." Jett dodged to one side and chuckled when Becka fisted her hands on her hips. "All in the past, darlin'. All in the past."

Becka went to sit on the arm of his chair. "Better be." She flexed a firm bicep. "I can body slam ya, ya know."

Envy shafted through Shannon when Jett yanked his wife across his lap, kissed her soundly, then sat her back up. "Woman, you're distracting me. Shannon has a serious problem that we can help with. Now quit trying to seduce me in front of company and let me talk."

The look of love between them filled the room with a warm glow. Shannon desperately wished she and Jackson shared that kind of emotion.

"Now where was I?" Jett asked. "Oh, yeah. Jackson's big mouth. Well, you see when he gets a little wasted, he talks. And here's the upshot. The man has some serious issues about his mother. Seems she abandoned him when he was about four. Just got up one day, packed her bags and drove off, leaving him alone in the house."

"Oh, no! He actually remembers that?"

"In minute detail. He kept expecting her to come back, even years after she'd left. But she never did. Later on he discovered that she had never wanted him in the first place. She'd gotten pregnant and married his dad, but had always felt trapped. One day she couldn't take it any longer."

"How did he find out such an awful thing?" Her heart broke for the child in Jackson that had felt so unwanted. She may have lost both parents but she knew from photos and baby books how cherished she'd been.

"When he was about ten or eleven he found his parents' marriage license, did a little subtraction with his birth date and figured it out. His dad told him the rest."

"Poor little kid." Shannon wrapped both arms around her belly. No wonder Jackson was so focused on their baby. He never wanted his child to suffer as he had.

"They heard through the grapevine where she'd gone," Jett said, "but he hasn't seen her since. His dad went nuts for a while, so his great-aunt quit her job and moved in to help out."

"That's why he's so close to Bonnie."

"He'd walk on razor blades for that woman. She gave up a very lucrative career and her social life to raise him. That's why he came back to Rattlesnake determined to pay off her mortgage when the bank threatened foreclosure."

"I didn't know about that either." It seemed there were a lot of things she didn't know about her husband. Things that made his behavior much more understandable.

Jett and Becka exchanged glances. "You do now."

No wonder he was in such a hurry to make his training clinics pay off. And no wonder he'd accepted Granddad's offer. He needed the money for Bonnie.

"So if Bonnie took such good care of Jackson, what are you trying to tell me? That nothing could compensate for the hurt his mother caused?"

Jett cocked a finger and pointed it at her. "You always were a smart one. Jacks is scared out of his mind of women. Oh, he's cool, like me." When both women snickered, he answered with a mock scowl. "But I've watched him for years. Any time a woman starts getting too close and he likes her too much, he backpedals. Gets the heck out of Dodge or sends them packing."

"He hasn't done either in this case," Shannon said.

"Kind of interesting, don't you think?"

"Not really. It only means that he sees no need. He's not in love with me."

"Wrong again. Gee, Shannon, you disappoint me. Jackson has a commitment problem. I know about those. Suffered a smidgen with one myself. He married you because he really, really wanted you, but deep inside he was afraid you would abandon him, too. So he jumped at this cockamamy idea of yours—and Gus's."

"Did he tell you this?" Shannon asked suspiciously. "Or are you making it up so I'll feel better?"

In truth, she did feel better. Just telling someone her troubles helped, though she doubted Jett's assessment of the situation.

"I think you should listen to him, Shannon," Becka said. "No one knows Jackson as well as Jett."

"I don't know...."

"Don't you owe it to yourself and your baby to find out?"

Shannon twisted the now-shredded tissue into a wad. What if they were right? What if there was a chance that she and Jackson could actually work something out?

"You've never been a quitter," Becka said softly.

Shannon hitched her chin. "I'm not the one quitting. Jackson is."

"He's there and you're here. I'd say you were the one who ran."

"I want what you and Jett have, the real thing, not a joke of a marriage filled with underhanded dealings."

Becka feigned amazement. "Is this the same friend of mine who went through three fiancés and had decided she never wanted to marry anyone?"

Something clicked inside Shannon's head. Before her marriage she'd only cared about the ranch, about work, but now she wanted more. In less than a year, her life had become totally enmeshed with Jackson's—and now with their baby's. Funny how love changed a person's focus.

"Okay. You're right. Both of you. If nothing else, Jackson and I need to lay all our cards on the table, to be completely honest with each other." With a disgusted huff, she shook her head. "Something I thought we'd done all along."

"Give the man a chance, Shannon," Jett said, bouncing up to offer a hand when she began rocking back and forth in an effort to lift her extra bulk from the soft sofa. "I'm serious. He's a little screwed up, but he's a good guy. Don't give up on him yet."

She squeezed his bicep in a silent thank you. "You're a pretty nice guy yourself."

He laughed. "Don't tell anyone. I have a reputation, you know."

Becka hooked an elbow in Shannon's and led the way to the door. "Come on, I'll walk you to your truck. Then I want you to go home and talk things out with that knot-headed, testosterone-imbalanced Cajun."

As Shannon bid her friend farewell and drove away, warm sunshine flooded the Texas landscape, but Shannon's heart remained heavy. Regardless of her friends' encouragement, she knew the truth. Jackson didn't love her. But even without the love she needed so badly, Shannon had to try to make a go of their marriage.

She patted the top of her belly. "You deserve a family, a mommy and a daddy. And I'll do everything I can to give you that. Even swallow my pride."

As good as Granddad had been to her, an empty space had always resided where her mother and daddy should have been. A child needed both. Wasn't Jackson proof of that?

The vast stretch of empty grassland between the remote Garret Ranch and her own home rushed past. Deep in thought, she processed vague images of fences and telephone poles, horses and cattle, but not another human being or house.

She reached toward the CD player.

A jackrabbit, as tall as a large dog, leaped from a grassy ditch.

Shannon knew better than to swerve, but instinct overcame reason. She jerked the wheel, felt the SUV skid away from her control. Electric shards of fear shot down her arms. The truck rocked, tipping threateningly onto two wheels and then plunged headfirst into the ditch.

The jolt slammed Shannon to the end of her seat belt and into the steering wheel just as the air bag deployed and propelled her backward against the headrest. The dual impacts knocked the breath from her. Something inside gave way and a hot gush of liquid flooded the seat.

Stunned, breathless and trembling, Shannon looked down. It took a minute before she realized what had happened.

"Oh, no. Please, God. Not my baby."

Mouth as dry as the Texas dirt, she restarted the SUV and tried to back out of the ditch. A cloud of dust enveloped her, filling up the interior. Tires spun until she smelled rubber, but the truck only rocked in place, refusing to budge.

A pain ripped from her back around to her belly. She bent forward, hands cradling the mound that was her baby.

"Not yet, baby. You're too little. Not yet."

But a deep cramping now joined the sharp pain.

She had to get out of here. To get help. She tried again to move the vehicle without success and wished she had remembered to grab her cell phone from the charger. Not that it would necessarily work out here, but in her distraught state and haste to leave the ranch, she hadn't even thought about the phone.

She shoved at the door, but getting out of the truck proved to be a challenge. Settled deep in the grassy dirt, the driver's door was pressed into the earth and wouldn't open. She crawled across the seat, stopping once while a cramp came and went, then managed to exit the passenger's door.

Climbing out of the ditch, she looked left and right down the highway. For as far as the eye could see, there was nothing. No houses, no vehicles, no farmers mowing hay.

Anxiety—or perhaps the nagging pain—made her sweat, though the day was not especially hot. Something was wrong. Something was very wrong.

She hadn't driven far, maybe five miles from Becka's, which meant the town of Rattlesnake—and a hospital—was still over thirty miles away.

The choice was clear. Setting her face toward the Garret Ranch, she started walking.

Five minutes into the walk, another contraction gripped her. She bent forward, held her baby and moaned but refused to stop. She had to keep moving. Becka was a nurse. She would know what to do.

The pain subsided and she tried to pick up speed, but the ache in her back and the hitch in her side nagged constantly.

Her shirt and jeans stuck to her body, soaked in sweat. Gnats buzzed around her head. And the heat seemed insufferable.

Nausea buoyed in her stomach and black spots danced before her eyes. Her knees threatened to buckle.

She wanted so desperately to lie down. But she had to keep shuffling onward. If she gave birth to a premature baby here, alone, they both could die.

* * *

Jackson paced the floor of his bedroom. Correction, the bedroom he shared with his pregnant wife. Over the months of their marriage she'd made some changes here and there. As he looked around, he realized how much she'd tried to make him feel at home, to please him. Gone were the frilly lavender curtains and bedspread, replaced by a burgundy plaid, or whatever that shade of reddish-purple was called. She'd rearranged the dresser and furniture, too, allowing room for his personal belongings. She'd even redecorated the walls with pictures of him working horses, had them blown up and framed to hang in a grouping on one wall.

This was no longer a woman's room. It was a couple's room. His and Shannon's. Though she'd never said the words again, every change spoke of her love for him. Shannon was like that. Her actions spoke loud and clear.

And now her actions said she was through with him. She'd left. Not that he hadn't expected it to happen eventually, but he'd thought he was insulated against that kind of disappointment. He'd thought wrong.

He paced to the dresser, picked up her perfume, opened it and breathed in. The scent of Shannon filled him. What should he do about her now that she knew his duplicity, now that she hated him?

He missed her. He wished she was here. He wished—

A startling revelation jerked through him. Raising his eyes to the mirror, he saw the answer in his own face.

"You idiot," he muttered to the stunned man in the mirror. He was the poor blind fool, not Gus.

Shannon was his wife, carrying his baby. No, she was more than his wife. She was his life. It was Shannon and her love that filled him, not horse training, not this ranch or any other. Only Shannon, and the child they'd made together. Gus was right. He was in love with the gorgeous, pain-in-the-butt woman. And she loved him. Or she had before today.

The lightning bolt of realization hit him again. Good grief almighty. He loved her.

But he'd hurt her, too. Badly.

Taking a Kleenex from the box on the dresser, he dabbed on the sweet scent of Shannon, folded the tissue and slid it into his shirt pocket.

By all that was holy, he'd make everything right again. He'd find a way to make her happy, to make her love him again. He'd give her everything he owned— granted that wasn't much now that he'd returned his share of the ranch to Gus, but someday he'd have more and Shannon could have it all. He'd even let her train horses her own way. He'd do anything except one—he wouldn't live without her.

But first he had to find her. To tell her how sorry he was and how much he loved her.

A quick telephone call confirmed his first guess. She'd gone to see Becka but was now on her way home. He considered waiting until she arrived, but nixed the idea. She was hurting, heartbroken, Becka said, because of him. He didn't want her to feel that way one more minute. He wanted to hold her now, to tell her the truth, to share his heart.

Grabbing his keys, he bounded down the stairs, climbed into the truck and was out of the driveway so fast he had to buckle his seat belt en route.

The drive was a long one. He'd likely meet her halfway.

Excitement rippled through his chest. Man, it felt good to be in love. To know what he really wanted out of life.

After passing through the city limits of Rattlesnake, he put the pedal down. Shannon would scold him for driving too fast, but the road was flat and empty. He would be able to spot her truck long before they actually met on the road.

Sure enough, he saw the red SUV from a distance, but instead of the joy he'd expected, black terror snaked down his spine.

"Shannon." Slamming on the brakes, he fishtailed to a stop. Shannon's SUV leaned to one side headfirst into a deep ditch.

Pulse hammering, he got out. "Shannon!" he called. "Are you okay?"

No answer.

Boots skidding down the incline, he glanced inside the SUV, but Shannon wasn't there. Then he saw the wet spot on the driver's seat and his heart stuttered to a standstill. It couldn't be what he feared. Shannon wasn't even eight months yet.

He searched all around the vehicle and, finding no sign of his wife, leaped into his truck and headed down the highway. She had to be up ahead somewhere, walking to find help. And if she was walking, she couldn't be in labor.

Could she?

In the far distance, beneath a blue sky with no clouds to filter the glaring sunlight, he spotted a form. A burst of relief energized him. He'd found her.

But as he drew nearer, he saw what he hadn't seen before. She was bent double, barely shuffling forward. Upon hearing the truck approach, she turned his way— and crumpled to the ground.

Jackson's mind exploded.

He thought he'd known fear before, but nothing in his life had ever scared him like this. His wife and his baby were in trouble. Bad trouble.

Slamming to a rocking halt, he catapulted out of the truck and rushed to where she lay in the dusty grass.

Her eyelids fluttered open. Relief filtered through the glazed blue depths.

"Jackson," she whispered. "The baby's coming."

Scooping her into his arms, he prayed as he'd never prayed before. She was quivering and drenched with sweat. Her clothes clung to her and her face was pale.

Jackson tenderly deposited her on the truck seat and then set off toward the Garret Ranch. A hospital would be better, but there was no time. She needed someone with medical training to be with her now. Becka was thirty miles closer than the nearest hospital.

"Hang on, darlin'," he murmured, trying to appear strong for her sake, though he was on the verge of losing his mind. "I'll get you to Becka. She'll know what to do."

A contraction hit her with a force that raised her off the seat. She'd no more than relaxed her white-knuckled fists than another slammed into her. This time she moaned, writhing from a pain that seemed too intense to Jackson. Not that he'd been with that many laboring women, but he'd birthed plenty of colts. Labor had a rhythm. What was happening to Shannon was chaotic.

"Something's wrong." Her voice shook. Shannon was boot-leather tough. And she'd lost one baby already. If she thought something was wrong, it was.

He rammed the accelerator to the floor and saw the speedometer climb higher until the truck floated over small bumps.

By the time he pulled into the Garret driveway, horn blasting, Shannon was uttering strange whimpering noises that scared him senseless.

As he gently lifted her from the truck, Becka and Jett rushed out the door.

"What's wrong?"

"She had an accident in the truck. The baby's coming."

Becka's sharp intake of breath reminded them all that the baby wasn't due for another six weeks. After a tense moment, the little nurse straightened her shoulders and allowed her medical training to blot out the fact that the laboring and possibly injured woman was her best friend.

"Jett, call an ambulance. Jackson, follow me. We'll prepare for the worst and hope for the best."

Jackson followed the tiny redhead into the house and down the long, cool hallway to a back bedroom. Becka yanked back the covers. "Put her here. I'll gather supplies."

Kneeling on the mattress edge, Jackson eased his wife onto the bed. Brushing his lips across her pale ones, he said, "I love you, darlin'. Hang tough. I love you."

"Our baby." She gripped her belly with both hands as though she could hold back the tide of nature. "Don't let him die."

Jackson's heart broke. "Don't worry, sweetheart. He's tough like you. He'll be okay." If only he believed his own words.

Becka, carrying a nurse's bag, a pile of towels and two clean bathrobes, returned just then.

Jackson levered upright. He towered over Shannon's small friend, but at this moment, she looked like a giant to him. His wife's life was in her hands. "I love her so much, Becka. Don't let anything happen to her."

Becka paused briefly in a flurry around the bed. "It's about time you figured that out."

Then she was back to work, helping Shannon undress, washing her down with a damp cloth, talking to her in a soft, professionally reassuring manner. Jackson followed the nurse's orders, helping smooth towels beneath Shannon's body.

Shannon arched her back and cried out for the first

time. She grabbed Jackson's arm in a death grip. "He's coming. Our baby. Don't let him die. Please. My baby."

Seized with unspeakable panic, Jackson cradled her face in his hands. "I love you, Shannon. Do you hear me? I love you and I'm not going to let anything happen to you or our baby."

The promise was not in his control and he knew it. Yet he had to make it.

Becka grabbed his arm and frowned a warning that said, "Don't scare her."

"Go in that bathroom there." She pointed at a door to his right. "Wash your hands with soap and warm water for two or three minutes. Wash all the way up to the elbows."

"Why?"

She looked at him as though he lacked reason. "I'm going to need your help."

He did as she commanded, reminding himself of all the colts he had delivered. This was no different. Nature would do the work. He would assist.

As he attacked his hands with soap, he noticed how his fingers shook. Who was he kidding? This was his baby. His wife. And they were in danger.

Refusing to give in to the pounding fear, Jackson dried his hands and returned to the bedroom. Becka held up one of the bathrobes. "Put this on to cover your clothes." She glanced at her patient. "Who knows where they've been, huh, Shannon?"

"Horse poop," Shannon said, trying to smile through

the sweat and pain. Jackson thought his heart would shatter with love for his brave woman.

"Be right back. Don't you two get frisky while I'm washing up." With a wink, Becka disappeared into the bathroom to wash her hands. Jackson marveled at her ability to remain so cool and calm on the outside, when she must be almost as frightened as he was.

Jackson snugged the robe around his waist and sat down on the edge of the bed, trying to be as cool as Becka. "How ya doing, babe?"

"Bellyache. Must have been something I ate." She gripped his hand as her belly undulated. "He's too small. It's too soon." And then her words were lost as she fought the wave of agony.

Becka sailed back into the room, took one look at Shannon and said, "Here we go."

Electricity shot up Jackson's spine.

Shannon's eyes widened. "No. Not yet."

But her body had a mind of its own.

In the next few minutes, with his heart bursting out of his chest and his stomach clenched in angst, Jackson sweat and strained along with his wife as nature took control.

When the smallest baby Jackson had ever seen slipped into the world, tears sprang to his eyes. Tears of joy. Tears of sorrow.

To his amazement, the tiny form opened her mouth, sucked in a breath and screamed herself pink.

Becka, face covered in perspiration, allowed a smile

as she wrapped the baby in a soft towel and laid her over Shannon's now flatter stomach. "You have a girl, Shan."

But Shannon didn't reply. Eyes closed, face pale, the new mother remained inert.

"Shannon." Jackson shook off the wonder of his daughter's birth to attend to his wife. "Darlin', can you hear me?"

He whirled toward Becka only to find her already wrapping Shannon's limp arm with a blood-pressure cuff. "Becka, what's wrong? What's happening?"

He'd thought the worst was over now that the baby had appeared, pink and crying. But he'd been wrong.

"Her pressure's too low." Tossing her stethoscope to one side, Becka gently scooted the newborn as high onto Shannon's chest as possible. "Baby looks okay for now. Grab those pillows. We need to elevate her legs, send more blood flow to the brain."

Jackson dove for the pile of throw pillows, afraid to ask, afraid not to. "She'll be okay, won't she?"

"I'm concerned about that accident. She must have sustained some internal injury." For once, the chipper nurse's expression was grim. She began massaging Shannon's abdomen. "Let's hope the ambulance arrives soon."

As though hit by a cannonball, Jackson fell on his knees at the bedside and poured out his soul to the woman he loved more than himself.

"Don't leave me, Shannon. I need you, baby. I love you." His voice broke, but he didn't care if Becka saw him weep. "I love you, I love you."

But Shannon didn't answer.

* * *

When the ambulance arrived and informed Jackson that he couldn't ride with Shannon to the hospital because of some cockamamy liability concern, they had a fight on their hands.

"That's what you think, buddy," he said, shoving his oversize body into the space next to Shannon and the baby. "Now somebody drive this thing."

Seeing the futility of arguing with a big, scared Cajun, the EMT shrugged and hopped aboard. The ambulance screamed away, IV swaying from the holder on the side of the vehicle.

All the way to the hospital, Jackson watched the clear liquid pouring into his wife and prayed it would make a difference. Over and over, he declared his love, kissing her face and her limp hands, smoothing her damp hair, not caring that the ambulance personnel witnessed his actions.

Once, eyes glazed, she roused to whisper, "My baby—" Then slipped away again before he could reassure her.

At the hospital, everything became a blur. Shannon and the baby were whisked away, leaving him to pace the waiting room like a rabid tiger.

A scrub-clad nurse shoved a surgical consent form under his nose and told him to sign. Shannon's OB doctor appeared and tried to talk to him, but Jackson's head roared so loudly nothing made sense. Thankfully, Becka and Jett had arrived by then and convinced him to sign the papers. He caught words like *hemorrhage* and *blood loss* that made his own blood run cold, but otherwise he was lost. Lost in fear for his wife and baby.

Stumbling to a plastic chair, Jackson dropped his head into his hands and prayed. From his shirt pocket rose the scent of Shannon's perfume. He removed the tissue and pressed it to his face.

Jett and Becka sat beside him, saying nothing, their presence more comforting than any words.

A hand clapped on his shoulder. Glancing up through blurry eyes, he saw Aunt Bonnie and Gus. Family. God, he needed family so badly right now.

His gaze locked on Shannon's granddad, the other man who loved her.

"I love her, Gus."

"I know, boy." The old man's face was drawn and strained.

"I didn't." And the notion angered him. Why hadn't he seen? Why hadn't he always been the man she needed, instead of a self-centered wrangler bent on going his own way? Why hadn't he accepted the love she so freely had given him? "I've been such an idiot."

"All men are idiots, Jackson." Aunt Bonnie slipped an arm over his shoulders and kissed his cheek. "Now that you know it, you can do something about it. Come on, now. Where's your faith? Shannon is made of strong stuff. She's going to be fine. Let's go see that new baby of yours."

Had he not been so distraught, Jackson would have grinned. Leave it to Aunt Bonnie to set him straight. "Can't. Have to wait for Shannon."

"Doc says they'll need about an hour. He'll find us when she's out of surgery."

"She'll be okay, won't she?" His question begged them all and no one let him down.

"You bet."

Following them up the elevator to the newborn nursery, Jackson stood in wonder in front of the window. His baby girl, with her skinny arms and legs and tiny pursed mouth, reminded him of a featherless bird. She lay naked inside an oxygenated Isolette, looking so helpless and fragile that he wanted to cry.

"She looks good for one so small," Aunt Bonnie said. "Why, I remember when Stella Duvall was born, they put her in a shoe box and set her on the oven door to keep warm. No fancy oxygen cribs back then, and she grew up to be the toughest woman in the bayou." She patted his arm. "This little one will be the same. Mark my word."

Torn between love for his daughter and fear for his wife, Jackson alternately watched the baby and the hallway, awaiting news that Shannon was out of surgery.

After an interminable amount of time in which he ate his entire stock of Dum-Dums and wore a path in the white hospital tile, word finally came, courtesy of a disembodied voice.

"Jackson Kane, please report to the second-floor nurses' station. Jackson Kane, to the second-floor nurses' station immediately, please."

The tension in his gut snapped and he bolted for the elevator.

Chapter Twelve

The dream had been so lovely, she didn't want to awaken. Jackson had told her he loved her. Not once but thousands of times, over and over until she'd wanted to laugh. But laughing hurt her stomach.

She frowned and tried to turn, but that hurt her stomach, too. What was wrong with her? Her body ached and she was so very tired.

In that half land between sleep and wakefulness, something clicked. She reached down to touch the place where her baby grew. Her arm, tangled in tubes of some kind, was useless. So she tried the other one, found it free, and laid it on her belly.

Her eyes snapped open.

In seconds, the ordeal flooded back in snatches and snapshots. The accident. Jackson's beloved face. He and Becka delivering the baby. The ambulance. And then the dreams that weren't dreams at all, but Jackson declaring his love over and over as though the words could save her.

Maybe they had. And maybe that's why he'd said them. Out of guilt and fear and compassion, but not out of love.

She had no idea how long she'd slept or what day it was, but she needed to know about her baby. Desperately.

Dragging the IV tube across her chest, she reached for the call button. Before she pressed it, someone spoke.

"Shannon?"

At the sound of the beloved voice, she raised her head, aware for the first time that she was not alone. An unshaven, bedraggled-looking Cajun sprawled in watchful exhaustion at the foot of her bed.

"My baby?" Her throat croaked as if she'd swallowed dry twigs.

With lithe movements, Jackson was off the bed and at her side in seconds. Dark eyes peered down at her through red rims. "Thank God. I thought I'd lost you."

His heartfelt words hardly registered. "My baby," she insisted, fear working its way along her nerve endings. "Where is she?"

"Our baby is fine. Our baby, Shan. Not yours, not mine, but ours. She's a beauty. Kind of small, but noisy and feisty like her mama."

His tired smile reassured her that their daughter really was all right. Great relief, like a tidal wave, washed over her.

"She came too early. But you saved us," she said simply, longing to stroke his whiskery cheek. He looked exhausted and beautiful and wonderful. She wished she could keep him forever.

Jackson denied her claim with a slow shake of his head. "You're the hero. Doc says your toughness pulled you through."

"I can't remember everything. It's all jumbled."

"The accident caused the placenta to tear instead of coming loose on its own. You were bleeding to death on the inside." He scraped a hand down his face. "If you hadn't delivered the baby when you did, neither of you would have made it. The surgery and two pints of blood turned you from a ghost to a human again."

"Two pints," she said in amazement. No wonder he looked so worried.

"You scared me to death, Shannon." He stroked the top of her hand with his thumb. "I thought I'd waited too late, that I'd lose you."

Her gaze flew to his. At the expression in his eyes, hope lifted like a swan in flight. "I didn't know you wanted to keep me."

"Oh, darlin', I want you so much I thought I'd die in that ambulance when you wouldn't wake up."

"Listen, cowboy, I'm real tired. Don't mess with my mind. If you're trying to say something, spit it out."

"Jett and Becka reamed me out good, told me how I'd hurt you. They said you were convinced I was staying married because of the baby and the ranch. Well, here's a news flash. I gave my share of the ranch back to Gus."

The blossoming hope broke into full flower. "You did?"

"Yeah." He grinned. "But I'm not giving the baby back. She's mine. And so are you." His face grew serious. "If you'll have me. If you can forgive me."

"Oh, Jackson. Oh, Jackson." Tears welled in her eyes. "You really meant all those I-love-yous." His voice had been raspy and frantic, wonderfully frantic.

He shifted from one boot to the other, uncomfortable, but pleased. "Thank God you heard me. I was afraid you couldn't, that I'd waited too long."

"I thought I was dreaming, but I heard every word."

"I meant every one of them."

"Then tell me again."

Dimples flashed in his weary face. "Sounds good to me, but this time I need to hold you, to touch you and know you're with me. Will I hurt you if I do?"

"You'll hurt me more if you don't." Carefully shifting her hips, she made room. Jackson eased his oversize body onto the bed and gently gathered her against him.

Nose to nose, exchanging heartbeats, Jackson said the words she'd longed to hear for months, perhaps years. "I love you, Shannon. With everything in me, I love you. Be my wife forever. Promise you won't leave me—ever."

Heart swelling with joy, Shannon stroked his cheek. The IV got in the way, but she didn't care. Jackson loved her. "You couldn't run me off with a horsewhip.

I love you, Cajun boy. I think I've loved you since I was eighteen years old."

"Yeah. Me, too." His finger made loving designs around her mouth, over the crease in her lips, down her chin. "We've finally come full circle, back to the place we should have always been. Together. And this time, we're staying."

He leaned in and replaced his finger with a kiss so tender Shannon wanted to weep.

When they parted, she whispered, "Say it again. Make me believe it."

"Glutton. I love you." He shifted and suddenly she smelled perfume.

She sniffed his shirt and asked teasingly, "Are you sure you spent the night at the foot of my bed?"

He pulled the tissue from his pocket and held it to her nose. "Yours. It was the only thing that kept me breathing last night while I awaited word on your condition."

A splash of love more powerful than any perfume resonated deep inside her. "Now I know you really love me."

"Well, just in case you need persuasion…" His lazy grin disappeared against her lips.

The door swooshed open, but Jackson went right on kissing his wife.

An amused female voice interrupted, "Excuse me, Mr. and Mrs. Kane, but you have an important visitor."

Reluctantly parting, Jackson levered up on one elbow but refused to get off the bed. He had Shannon in his arms, safe and sound, and he planned to stay that way for a while.

"Who is i—?" he started to ask, but the words died in his throat. The nurse held a tiny, pink-wrapped bundle against her ample bosom.

Shannon sucked in a delighted breath. "My baby."

"Ours," he growled and received a weary smile for the effort. "Put her here," he instructed, patting the narrow space between himself and Shannon. "Mama and I both want to inspect her."

The grinning nurse did as he asked. "I'll be back to get her in about fifteen minutes. Mommy needs her rest and baby needs to be in the Isolette for a couple of more days, but Dr. Dean thought seeing her would be good for Mrs. Kane."

"Dr. Dean is right." Shannon's fingers shook as she peeled back the blanket to gaze upon the perfectly round face of her daughter. "Oh, my precious."

They counted her toes and fingers, marveled over the shock of black hair, stroked the button nose and laughed when she grimaced.

"She's so perfect. So beautiful."

"Her skin is as soft as a horse's muzzle," Jackson murmured.

"Leave it to us to compare her to a horse." Shannon folded the petal-soft blanket over the baby and kissed her smooth forehead. "She needs a name. We've never talked about that."

"My fault."

"No more blame." Shannon laid a finger across his lips. "Now is what matters. And right now our baby girl needs a name."

Maybe they hadn't discussed it, but he'd done some thinking on the topic. Even he knew a baby had to be named, no matter how pigheaded her daddy was. "How do you feel about Bailey?

"Bailey?" Shannon tried it out, her tired eyes lighting up. "Yes, Bailey. I love it. Bailey Suzanne Kane."

A ripple of pleasure moved through Jackson as he understood his wife's intent. "Suzanne is Aunt Bonnie's middle name."

"I know. What do you think?"

"I think," he whispered, "I'm the luckiest man on earth."

Clutching Shannon's hand, he leaned across his daughter to kiss his wife. A lump rose in his throat. The woman, the baby. God, he loved them. Why had it taken him so long to realize that this was what life was really about? Two people who loved each other and made a family together. Two people who shared their plans and dreams, as he and Shannon had done for months. Two people who came through the storms stronger and better.

He watched the play of emotions on his wife's beautiful face. She had to be tired and sore and weak, but the glow radiating from her lit the dark places in his heart. She was amazing, his Shannon.

"All my life I wanted a whole family," she murmured softly.

"Me, too."

"And now we have one."

Filled to the brim, he exhaled a long sigh of contentment.

If he never became a successful horse whisperer, he knew one thing. The most important success of his life was right here, right now, in his arms. And if he never trained another horse, he'd still have all he needed—his wife, his baby and a lifetime of love.

* * * * *

*Look for Linda Goodnight's next
Silhouette Romance, PRINCE INCOGNITO,
on sale April 2006!*

COMING NEXT MONTH

#1802 DOMESTICATING LUC—Sandra Paul
PerPETually Yours
Puppy's got his work cut out for him when he meets his new owner, Luc Tagliano. Though grieving his lost mistress, Puppy wants this thickheaded human to see how good regular playdates with kind and patient animal trainer Julie Jones could be....

#1803 HONEYMOON HUNT—Judy Christenberry
When he hears that his wealthy father is globe-trotting with some new bride, Nick Rampling senses a gold digger's snare and teams up with Julia Chance, the bride's prim daughter. But their cat-and-mouse hunt for the couple soon convinces him it's *their* hearts that are in flight!

#1804 A DASH OF ROMANCE—Elizabeth Harbison
Run out of her catering gig by an evil queen of a boss, Rose Tilden relocates to a neighborhood Brooklyn diner. But when the handsome developer Warren Harker shows interest in the area, she learns that even the chaotic stirrings of love can create intoxicating flavors....

#1805 LONE STAR MARINE—Cathie Linz
Men of Honor
How could ex-marine captain Tom Kozlowski mistake her for a stripper-gram? Feisty schoolteacher Callie Murphy's anger cools when she sees the pain in his eyes. And as she reaches out to this wounded warrior, she's soon wondering if he can't teach *her* something powerful about the human heart....

SRCNM0106